Books by M K Scott

Cupid's Catering Company
Culinary Cozy Mystery
Wedding Cake Blues
Truffle Me Not
Double Chocolate Deception

The Talking Dog Detective Agency
Cozy Mystery

A Bark in the Night
Requiem for a Rescue Dog Queen
Bark Twice for Danger
The Ghostly Howl
Dog Park Romeo
On St. Nick's Trail

The Painted Lady Inn Mysteries Series
Culinary Cozy Mystery

Murder Mansion
Drop Dead Handsome
Killer Review
Christmas Calamity
Death Pledges a Sorority

Caribbean Catastrophe

Weddings Can be Murder

The Skeleton Wore Diamonds

Death of a Honeymoon

Cakewalk to Murder

Sailors Take Warning

Two Many Sleuths

The Way Over the Hill Gang Series

Cozy Mystery

Late for Dinner

Late for Bingo

Late for Shuffleboard

Late for Square Dancing

Late for Love

Late for the Wedding

Late for the Wedding

By

M K Scott

To Larriane

Editor and friend

Chapter One

A BREEZE CAUGHT a tumbling, golden leaf and twirled it toward two chairs that sat smack dab on the emerald lawn. A bald pate, sunglasses, and overlarge ears, reminiscent of a house-elf, graced the man already seated there. Herman Fremont claimed the other seat and settled into it with a sigh.

The leaf continued its descent, landing delicately atop the elf lookalike's head. Gus Randall brushed the leaf off and spoke. "Early fall for Southern Indiana. What do you think, Herman?"

Herman glanced at the late afternoon blue sky and cotton ball clouds, and then spoke. "Can't complain about the weather."

"Remember when we worked on the case of the veteran with the little dog?"

A raspy chuckle served as an answer. "We were almost crushed by a wrecking ball. How could I forget?"

"Me, either." Gus snort-laughed and pressed a hand to his chest. "Got my heart pumping."

"Same here."

Pulling his sunglasses down, Gus blinked and said, "You know…"

Before Herman could inquire about the nature of the unfinished statement, a car door slammed nearby, drawing their attention to the parking lot that encircled Greener Pastures Assisted Living

Community rather like a moat. At least that's the way Herman thought of it when driving off the grounds to investigate a cold case. The woods that encircled the rambling brick building on two sides added to the air of isolation.

A nearby residential neighborhood, composed of ranches and two-story homes, along with a major road not too far away, gave the lie to the impression. On a quiet day like today, traffic served as white noise. Technically, Herman could leave the grounds, but Gus could not. Questionable shenanigans had his family placing him at the home for his own good, treating him more like a child than a capable adult. Catch something on fire and people go crazy.

A forty-something man approached, sporting a close to the skull haircut, sharp knife-pleated khakis, and a starched white oxford shirt. He waved when he spotted Gus and Herman.

"Morning, Ron!" Herman called out while Gus snapped a quick salute.

"Morning," Ron called back and grinned, crinkling the scar that slashed across his face making him look a little less like the loser in a knife fight. "I appreciate you two taking the perimeter guard." As he normally did, Ron good-humoredly solicited information from the two veterans. "Any intruders?"

"No, sir," Gus answered. "Only a few ducks near the ornamental pond, but that's to be expected."

"Good job, Sergeant. Carry on." He sketched a brief salute and then walked to the center's double front doors and proceeded inside.

Herman grumbled. "Today was *my* day to report—you knew that."

"Your loss." Gus smirked and said, "Gotta be quick. Not surprising since your tour of duty tended to be the leisurely sort. Better luck tomorrow."

Used to having his wartime duty of guarding a vital canal disparaged, Herman chose not to even address the comment. Instead, he promised himself he'd find an opportunity to talk to Ron. Once he did, he'd hold that over his buddies at lunch. Maybe he'd find out the origin of the scar. *That* would impress.

Jake Simpson, Gus Randall, and Herman Fremont met during boot camp and had kept in touch over the decades. It could be their shared service that caused admiration for the center's newest director. More likely, the fact that he treated each resident like an actual person as opposed to a source of revenue earned it. "I'll be ready next time. Just you wait and see."

Instead of answering, Gus tucked a white wireless earbud into his ear and leaned back into his chair. Unlike Herman, Gus apparently enjoyed the leisurely pace their lives assumed. No wonder Gus ignored most of his earlier conversation. He couldn't hear him. He occasionally made a remark, but nothing pertinent. At best, he probably reacted to seeing Herman move his lips. Just to test his theory, Herman mouthed silently, *the walrus shoots pool after midnight.*

Gus pulled out his earplugs, slid his sunglasses down his nose to expose his eyes, and arched his eyebrows. "I know you aren't saying anything."

"How? Don't tell me you couldn't hear me because you've ignored most of what I said this morning. Do you even know what they're serving for lunch today?" Herman threw out the question, well aware their conversations ran toward extreme predictability of late.

"Oven baked chicken with mashed potatoes and gravy, glazed carrots, and blueberry muffins. Chocolate cake."

He got it right. Maybe Gus heard more than he thought. His brow lowered as he considered the possibility of being wrong—not an action he engaged in overmuch. Often, Gus acted as if he couldn't hear, blaming it on his time as an explosive ordnance specialist. Still, other times he heard just fine, especially when someone tried to get something by him.

Gus leaned forward to poke at his friend. "I had you going. My gal, Eunice, made a point of reading the menu to me. She loves her baked goods and is afraid they might run out. Warned me not to be late for lunch. Anyhow..." he pushed his sunglasses on top of his head, extracted a small case from his pocket, and placed his earbuds inside. He brandished the case. "Handy things. My grandson bought them for me. Great for listening to podcasts." He reached into his pocket, pulled out his phone, and fiddled with it.

"Podcasts?" He'd heard plenty of the staff members discuss their favorite podcast. "You?"

"Oh yeah." Gus gave an enthusiastic nod. "There's all kinds. Tons of true crimes and cold case ones, too." His bushy eyebrows lifted as he continued, "Some of the folks who actually solve the cold cases aren't even detectives. They call themselves Internet Sleuths. A crime might catch their interest and they keep turning it over, looking for angles, suspects, and motivations long after the locals shelved it. Apparently, they can find everything on the Internet from photos to information about suspects, and even listen to 911 calls."

That piqued his interest. Even though he and Gus were the only folks on the front lawn, Herman leaned closer. "With Marcy being back in the office, not many cold cases come our way anymore."

"True," Gus agreed, glanced back at the building, and bent at the waist to close the space between them. "Even though we tried to keep our involvement hush-hush, the higher-ups must have heard and put the kibosh on things. We civilians, not that we're ordinary folk, but civilians just the same, must have embarrassed them."

It might be a possibility, however, not a strong one. Herman doubted the local police worried a handful of senior citizens might tarnish their image and sniffed his probable summation. "You know, work probably piled up while Marcy convalesced here. Don't forget the budding romance between her and her former partner, Lance."

"You got that right." Gus giggled, then winked. "Those two youngsters are on the right side of fifty-one. I expect there's all sorts of wooing going on, including picnics in the park, long drives in the country on a Sunday afternoon, and even taking in a drive-in movie or two."

Herman tried to remember what he did as a young man and couldn't remember any of those things. After returning from war, he discovered his only sister had married and moved to Ashville, which left just his parents. His sweetheart decided not to wait for him due to the fact he might not make it back. She also felt the need to point out he could be a selfish bore. Never confident, this caused him to shy away from dating, afraid some other woman might share the same sentiments. "Not sure couples do that stuff anymore."

"You may be right. Cold cases brought Eunice and me together."

"Hear ya," Herman commented, and then coughed, trying to clear his throat.

"It gave my life purpose." Gus pushed back his shoulders and then allowed them to droop as he continued, "Now it's like before Marcy showed up here."

There was another throaty rumble and another cough before Herman managed a slight smile. "You're right." He stared off in the direction of the parking lot. "There's got to be a few mysteries that need solving."

Gus glanced at his watch, stood, and patted his companion's shoulder. "You go find us a juicy case. I got a date with my gal. We're part of a trivia team. Our specialty is serial killers."

"Of course it is." Herman waved to his friend and then continued to speculate on his current dilemma. The only cold cases they received came via Lance, Marcy's partner. With no Marcy at the center, Lance failed to come by with armfuls of cold cases to interest the recovering detective, which meant he'd have to dig up his own unsolved mystery.

A loud boom erupted behind Herman, resulting in his jumping to his feet, placing a hand on his racing heart, and turning toward the center as bits of wood, shingles, and drywall showered him and the lawn. Gus lay prone on the ground with his hands covering his head. Not thinking twice about the noise and its origin, Herman dashed as much as his stiff knees would allow to his friend's side. "Are you okay?" He gasped the words as he lowered himself beside his friend.

Gus lifted his head, shaking off a shingle particle, and asked, "Are we being bombed?"

Using his flattened hand as a sun-shield, Herman peered at the sky. "No planes in sight."

There was no word of reproach for his friend who automatically assumed enemy fire. Complacency delivered many a soldier to an early grave. The words uttered years ago by his drill sergeant returned. Observe the area and check for the slightest thing awry. Herman stared at the single-story, rambling building with the gable roof.

Herman offered his hand to help Gus up, which he took. They both stood and hugged tightly, patting each other on the back. After a few seconds, they separated and delivered half-hearted shoulder punches to each other.

"I don't know what got into me," Herman muttered, running a hand over his face. "I saw you on the ground and I thought…" He paused and shook his head. "Oh, never mind."

Gus inhaled deeply and said, "Me, too."

Nothing more needed to be said by the two veterans. They turned in unison to study the roof. A dirty gray smoke clouded the sky, pouring from the ragged, blackened hole that hadn't been there seconds before.

Gus pushed down his sunglasses and squinted. "What do you think happened?"

Well aware his friend refused to wear glasses because it might make him look old, Herman wondered how much he could distinguish. After taking an audible breath, Herman admitted, "I have no clue, but I think we were just handed our next mystery. We need to round up the troops."

Chapter Two

THE AUTUMN SUN spotlighted the debris littering the grass. After the deafening boom, a heavy silence lay over the grounds until the front double doors of the center banged open. Sound stampeded out along with the uniformed staff, who kept shouting orders as they ran back and forth, acting like sheepdogs as they attempted to herd the confused residents in the correct direction. An acrid stench of motor oil and burnt fabric hung in the air, delaying the evacuation as residents slowed and fanned the air in front of them.

"Keep going," a sizable female employee, garbed in a cartoon smock that hinted at a playful personality, shouted. She pointed at a thin line of ornamental trees that served as a barrier between the center and the nearby neighborhood. "Head toward the Bradford Pear trees!"

The majority of residents complied without a peep, moving as fast as they could go. As children, they must have listened to their teachers and made their parents proud. Not all of the residents qualified as rule followers, however.

One slender woman with a still firm chin turned to address the shouting aide.

"Is this a drill?" Eunice Ledbetter's shrill voice carried over the hubbub. "I hate these stupid fire drills."

A continual *beep, beep, beep* of an alarm carried across the parking lot as doors opened on different wings, emitting a steady parade of bewildered residents and agitated employees. The local fire department's ladder truck's brakes squealed as it made a hard right into the parking lot, attracting attention. The exasperated aide in the cartoon smock, probably never guessing she'd be shepherding reluctant residents to safety when she woke this morning, pointed to the fire truck. Her harsh tone conveyed her tension. "Does that *look* like a drill?"

Eunice swung her attention from the woman to the fire truck and back to the woman again. "It could be a trick question. A while back, firefighters showed up for a grease fire. And when a dryer caught on fire because the lint collector was full, they came then, too."

"Go on!" the woman shouted. "My job is to make sure you don't burn up. It's not going to happen if you keep asking questions."

"Geesh!" Eunice huffed and then moved to where some residents in wheelchairs and a few taking a break on their walker seats, along with the uniformed staff, waited along the edge of the property. A few even broke into applause as the firefighters arrived, confident that whatever happened would be put right due to the efforts of the courageous first responders.

Herman and Gus stayed in the middle of the green lawn, well away from the other residents.

"That's a dirty gray smoke," Gus commented as both he and Herman continued to stare at the smoke as it moved upward and then dissipated as the breeze hit it.

Excited chatter, along with staff calling out residents' names, provided background noise together with the whoop of another emergency vehicle arriving. Herman moved closer to his friend, the better to talk privately. "What's up with the smoke color?"

Instead of answering, Gus held out his hand. Understanding what his friend wanted, Herman took off his glasses and handed them to Gus. "You really are going to have to break down and get your own pair. It's not good using someone else's glasses. Hurts your eyes."

A grunt served as his response. Gus held the glasses up and peered through them before speaking. "Yep, it's what I thought. Dirty gray."

"Yeah, you already said that." Herman shook his head. Now and then his friends would make a cryptic comment. Sometimes, he figured they thought they'd said something else, but failed to actually say the words. Other times, they said it like, duh, everybody knows what *that* means. At those times, he chose to say nothing.

Gus handed back his glasses. "Thanks. As for me getting glasses, I don't need them. I don't drive. When it comes to reading, what I can't decipher, Eunice can. The woman has eyes like a hawk." He chuckled. "Talons, too. Never cross her."

"I try not to." Herman had a brush or two with the acerbic busybody, but she usually saved her razor wit for his own sweet bride, Lola. Even though it made no sense, he'd swear the two women enjoyed exchanging barbs. Lola, a former Vegas showgirl, knew how to defend herself just fine.

"Smoke…" Herman prompted, afraid the topic got sidetracked by the mention of his friend's gal pal. Love tended to do that, no matter what the age.

"It's not white smoke, that's for sure." Gus mumbled something indecipherable.

"Excuse me?" Herman canted his head as if that would enable him to hear better in spite of the chaos happening around them. One of the female custodians, dressed in a chambray work shirt with a Greener Pastures logo and waving her hands, jogged toward them.

"You're too close! You've got to move. There might be another explosion."

Gus huffed and shot Herman a knowing look as he followed the woman, talking as he did so. "There won't be another explosion. It wasn't a gas explosion. Nope." He gave an emphatic shake of his head. "High-explosive smoke. Not the bright white smoke you see with black powder."

Herman followed closely, not wanting to miss a word of the summary. If anyone would know about explosives, Gus would. Of course, his information might veer toward the dated, unless he kept up with innovations.

The custodian delivered them to another staff member who held an electronic tablet and then announced, "Two more lost lambs for you."

Lambs, indeed! The label caused him to glare at the woman's back as she moved away. Sometimes, the younger they were, the less they realized that older folks had just as much on the ball as anyone else—maybe more, since they remembered stuff as opposed to looking it up on their phones.

"Your names?" the staff member, whose oversized nametag shouted *AIDE* in 20pt font letters below her name, inquired.

"Herman Fremont."

She located it on her screen, swiveled her head to peer at Gus, and made a small huff. "Oh, Gus I know."

Everyone knew Gus in some form or fashion, which worked against him at times. This might be one of those times. Her eyes narrowed and her mouth pursed a bit before she spoke. "Were you in the building just now?"

Herman knew where this might be heading without resorting to his normal sleuthing methods. "No, he was with me. We were talking about podcasts."

The lifted, penciled-in eyebrows telegraphed doubt. Gus decided to solidify his whereabouts by adding, "True crime podcasts. *My Favorite Murder* is one of my favorites. Have you heard that one?"

She huffed and then scrolled down her tablet while mumbling. "Must be nice to have endless free time to listen to podcasts."

Gus's alert expression and half-opened mouth meant he heard. No doubt he could rattle off a dozen podcasts he enjoyed. Not so with Herman—he knew how to avoid attention. Sometimes, he thought he could be a world-class spy with the way he blended into the woodwork. "Are we done here?" he inquired with a bland expression, masking his impatience to slip away somewhere quieter to discuss what they'd just witnessed.

"Yes." She gestured to a large group of residents mingling at the edge of the property. "Take your place over there."

"Of course," Herman agreed and grabbed his friend's arm to tow him along. Not happy with the situation, Gus complained as they headed toward the golden-leafed trees. "We need to find our women. What about Jake?"

"Yoo-hoo! Over here!" Eunice's shrill voice pierced the chatter.

One down and three to go. A little away from the rest of the mob, near a maple tree, Herman recognized the curvaceous shape of his bride, Lola. Nearby his wife, a slender brunette stood beside a tall, dark-haired male. It had to be Hannah Holt and Jake Simpson. No one else at the center had such artificially black hair. Jake even got praise on the hue from a few of the evening employees who liberally employed black eyeliner and nail polish. He released his grip on Gus but made sure to point to where the others stood. "Meet us over there. We need to come up with a plan."

Chapter Three

GREENER PASTURES ASSISTED Living Facility actually boasted a couple of acres of smooth grass as the name indicated. The tall trees provided a serene backdrop, if you overlooked the flashing emergency lights. Currently, fire fighters jumped from the truck and unloaded equipment while the evacuees watched with interest from a safe distance while speculating on the cause of their exit.

Herman headed toward the maple trees when another high-pitched siren whined and then sputtered to a stop as a patrol car entered the parking lot. Normally, Herman would have rubber-necked like the rest of the residents who pivoted to view the newest visitor. Voices shouted, "What's going on? Did you hear anything? I'm missing out on the trivia contest!"

The last voice undoubtedly belonged to Eunice. As for the rest, if anyone bothered to answer their inquiries, no one would hear due to the fire department's diesel engine truck rumbling nearby. The ruckus pulled folks out of their homes across the way in the nearby neighborhood. Most stood on their porch stoops, focused on Greener Pastures, and made no effort to be discreet. Perhaps they exited their homes to see what set their dogs barking. If he took a charitable view, the neighbors might be waiting for a sign to dash over and help. School must be on fall break because two youngsters rode their bikes to the edge of the property—not bold enough to enter, but close enough to report back to their parents.

In the bedlam of emergency vehicles arriving, a few vehicles slipped out, including a large boxy uniform delivery truck and a dark blue SUV. Firefighters jogged toward the center doors decked out with compressed air tanks. The leader gripped a fire ax. Add in about a hundred or so residents with more than a handful with diagnosed hearing issues standing outside, trying to uncover information by yelling, and only worsened the problem. Whenever a person resorted to screaming questions, their blood pressure spiked along with their temper.

Nope, he'd resist the temptation to glance over his shoulder. Never a fan of the loud and chaotic, he continued his stroll toward the maple trees and the serenity they epitomized. Their outstretched branches welcomed him and offered sanctuary.

Lola, his new bride, spotted him and using her three-footed cane, hurried to meet him. The cane represented her hurry to leave the facility along with her desire to remain a fashion diva. She joked that her walker shouted *elderly*, while the cane hinted at rehab after an adventurous mishap. His elegant wife set the tone for the center with her manicured nails and perfect coiffure. Advancing years made no dent in her beauty routine. She commented that older women needed all the help they could get, and she wasn't reluctant to take it, either. Her outspokenness and appearance also earned her some enemies—not that she cared.

He picked up his pace, wanting to save his beloved a few steps. When they met on the parking lot blacktop, they exchanged a brief kiss. Simple physical contact awakened a delayed thought. "Oh, my sweet!"

He carried his wife's hand to his lips and kissed it. He spoke with fervency, "I'm not sure what I would have done if I'd lost you."

Lola placed her hand on his cheek and gave him a tender look. "You haven't." She dropped her hand and gestured to the couple standing a few feet away. "Come join us at the tree. Hannah's asking if it's like this all the time."

"Is she frightened?" As one of the newest sleuths and a recent resident, the poor woman must be beside herself.

"Ha!" Lola wrinkled her nose and chuckled. "Just when I think you might be getting more progressive, you go and make some remark like that. Not every woman is a damsel in distress."

It was not the first time they'd had this discussion. Maybe women entered careers today that fifty years ago would be unthinkable, but that didn't stop him from trying to play the gentleman. Call him old-fashioned, but he tried to help the fairer sex whenever he could. Whether it consisted of holding a door open or offering a compliment, he did it. Sure, his upbringing included chivalric gestures, but he tried a little harder just to lose that selfish bore label he'd picked up as a returning soldier.

He held out his crooked arm for his wife, which she took with a tender look. "I have to admit, I rather like being treated like a fragile creature. Back when I was twenty, about three-quarters legs and working hard to earn myself a place as a full-time dancer, no man ran ahead to make things easier for me."

"None?" He shook his head slowly. "There must have been a bunch of stupid men out there in Vegas."

"A lot of muscle—not much brains. Just as well..." Lola wrinkled her nose. "None of the other girls would have taken me seriously. I had to go through a boot camp of sorts and learn how to

16

not only balance a twenty-pound helmet of rhinestone and feathers on my head, but I also had to do it in three-inch heels and walk up and down stairs gracefully during a number. We even had to learn to fall properly so as to not attract attention to ourselves or cause a domino effect."

"Oh, that would have been something to see." Herman waggled his brows, aware such a comment would not go unremarked upon.

"It would be a pink slip for sure and no chance of getting another showgirl position. At five-foot-eight and not having the benefit of ballet lessons, I was always the most likely to be cut from a line. Good thing I got out when I did."

Even though Lola insisted that keeping up her appearance came from her short stint as a showgirl, she never really talked about it. It was odd she had become so chatty all of a sudden. Before they pulled even with Hannah and Jake, he decided to delve a little deeper. "I've seen your photos. You had to be one of the most beautiful showgirls at that time."

Color painted her cheeks as she patted Herman's arm affectionately. "You're sweet. However, as a showgirl, you're supposed to blend in with all the other girls, rather like the Rockettes."

"I'll take your word for it. I imagine you had young bucks trying to chat you up every night."

Lola stopped, causing him to halt, and then turned to face her husband. "I do believe you're jealous."

"A little." His eyes dropped to the ground as he continued, "I wouldn't have stood a chance."

"It wouldn't have been due to a lack of charm and a headful of fabulous hair," she teased and tugged his arm to continue walking.

Herman used his free hand to smooth his thick silver hair that he allowed to touch his collar, resulting in a few of the residents calling him a *hippie*. "If you think I have thick hair now, you should have seen me then. I had to get a haircut almost every week just to keep it under control." Their steps carried them to within hearing range of the other two. Jake reacted first.

"Don't tell me you're regaling the poor woman with tales of your thick hair. I'm sure she's heard plenty by now. We've got more important things to yammer about."

Someone who didn't know them might think they didn't get along, but their mild joking served as their bonding ritual as opposed to deep, heart-to-heart talks about the meaning of life. Still, Herman tried to give back as much as he got. "I guess you want to talk about *your* hair and how it manages to get darker every day. Back when we were in boot camp, wasn't it a dishwater blond?"

"Good heavens, no! You must be thinking of Gus." Jake crossed his arms and frowned, a muscle twitching near his left eye.

Anxious to cover the awkward moment, Hannah gestured toward the building. "I think it's a gas explosion."

"It could be," Lola agreed. "I first thought it was the kitchen or the laundry. There's been more than one smoke alarm triggered by both." The group exchanged knowing looks as each person expounded on what could have caused the fire.

Jake pushed his hands into his pockets and shifted his weight, drawing attention, and then waited a couple of seconds before actually speaking, for the maximum benefit. It was easy to understand why he'd made a career out of sales. "I figure it has something to do with the new wing they're adding. How about you, Herman? What's your opinion?"

His free hand went back to rub his neck. Until now, he'd just reacted. Not many things blew up in their town. Workers at the local quarry created contained explosions, but that was about it, except for the occasional gas leak. Gus mentioned something about it being a bomb, but having worked in explosive ordnance, he thought everything had to do with explosives.

"Well," he started, searching his mind for things that went boom unexpectedly. "There's water heaters, the furnace boiler—even clouds of flour can catch fire."

There were some murmurs of agreement. Herman inhaled deeply, knowing he'd rip away any reassurance his explanation may have offered with his next sentence. "The problem is the hole blown in the roof isn't anywhere near a boiler, water heater, or even the dietary area."

"What about individual kitchens?" Hannah offered shyly, perhaps not feeling entirely part of the group.

"You plan on doing much baking here?" Lola asked with a smirk.

"Nope. Didn't do much at my old home. Not sure why I would here. Kitchens here are basic. I'm not sure a full-size baking sheet could fit inside the oven. Besides, we have a dining room, and they have decent food. Why cook?"

"Exactly," Lola agreed and bobbed her head. "Personal kitchens are a no. That leads us to what?"

Herman shrugged. "I have no clue. Maybe we should let the professionals do their job."

"Oh really?" Lola purred the words as her eyes met her husband's. "I'm not against letting the professionals do their thing." She cocked her head flirtatiously, then tapped one finger against his forearm. "It wouldn't hurt if we took a gander. It's not every day we're delivered our very own mystery."

Chapter Four

FLASHING LIGHTS FROM the emergency vehicles, along with the constant movement of the first responders and staff members, created a mosaic of both sound and color against the Indian Summer late morning. Taking advantage of the chaos, the sleuths launched their information-gathering mission.

Gus took the lead. He turned, held a finger to his lips, pointed to the far end of the parking lot, and waved everyone forward as if in a spy movie. They crept half-crouched, using cars for cover as they made their way to H Wing.

The SUVs and jacked-up trucks worked best since they allowed the opportunity for the sleuths to straighten and stand upright. Once they cleared the lot, the group hustled as best they could to the shadow of the building. A long line of pine trees shielded their activity from curious neighborhood gawkers. With no one in the building with the exception of firefighters, it should be safe to pass the windows as long as they moved with the stealth of a hunting tiger.

Eunice stumbled, bumping into Gus, startling him, and resulting in a few words better left unsaid. His face blanched with the realization of his verbal slip. Herman pointed to the flashing fire alarm mounted on the side of the building. As it pulsed, it continued to blare a teeth-gritting signal that somehow had become normal in the last twenty or so minutes between now and the explosion. Inhaling deeply, he nodded at his friend, who led the way to the new construction. Its unalarmed, camera-less doors made it easy to avoid detection when leaving on a cold case mission. The hardcore staff smokers made use of it, too. Only today, they'd be out front with everyone else wanting to light up, but unable to due to their job and not wanting to be seen with a lighter, especially after an explosion. Anyone with a lighter earned a second look—and not the good kind.

A couple of pallets of bricks, wood chunks, and sawdust marked the new construction area. Knowing that footprints left in the sawdust in this off-limits area could raise suspicion, Gus tiptoed leaving only half prints. The other sleuths followed his example, except for Lola, who moved forward wiping away any discernable prints by whipping her cane across the prints. Anyone who recognized the cane impressions would assume that a disoriented resident had wandered the wrong way. Since old people so seldom garnered notice and almost never for criminal acts, a crime lord could rule from a motorized scooter without attracting attention. Oddly, most people glanced away when spotting a disabled individual as if a physical disability could be passed on like a cold.

The scent of stale cigarette smoke permeated the air and testified to previous smokers. Even though it might be a long shot, Gus reached for the door handle. It swung open. His eyebrows arched as a sense of triumph rushed through him. Thank goodness for the smoking staff at Greener Pastures. He held the door wide as the sleuths paraded in with expressions ranging from surprise to amusement. They huddled in the hall to plan their next action since even making it this far had ranked as an impossibility.

"Where to next? I'm not sure how this fact-gathering mission works," Hannah asked with a shrug. "All my previous research came from books, the occasional true crime show, and the Internet."

Gus pondered the inquiry. "Do we *have* a system? Usually, we argue about approaches and end up trying the most do-able ones."

Possibly not satisfied with his reply, Eunice took it upon herself to clarify. "We should go to the administration office since that's where the explosion occurred or thereabouts."

A gentle murmur of voices ensued as they weighed the feasibility of such a plan, which served as the arguing phase. A burgundy nail-tipped hand shot up, drawing attention to its owner, Lola. Well aware of the power of a dramatic pause, she waited until all eyes turned her way and only the blare of the fire alarm sounded in the distance. Fortunately, the fire alarms usually ended up as the last item installed on new construction. "You do realize the firefighters will be in that area checking out the room."

"Good point," Hannah agreed with a head bob but continued speaking. "We have the firefighters today. The folks who point the hoses and rescue pets. The arson investigators will show up later, possibly tomorrow."

"Maybe," Herman inserted, but his furrowed brow said otherwise. "I suspect the fire marshall is on his way for a looksee. The ATF or FBI could show up, depending on what the fire marshall finds."

"Not good," Jake said as he raked his hand through his unnaturally black hair. "There will be people swarming everywhere. We need to get in there now or at best, walk by and get a peek." He pivoted to peer down the hall. "No one in sight here."

"Duh." Eunice grimaced. "No reason for them to be here."

Rather than respond, Jake continued to glance down the hallway, shifting his weight from foot to foot.

"Okay," Hannah said, making eye contact with each sleuth, except for Jake, who had his back to everyone while on the lookout. "I assume our plan is to head toward the office area. What do we do if we're stopped?"

A giggle sounded and Eunice held up her hand. "I've got this. As you may have noticed, people assume older folks are somewhat lacking in intelligence. They assume any hesitation in speech, any wrong word signals dementia." She crinkled her nose. "Now, if someone on the good side of forty does the same, it's no big deal. When in places we shouldn't be, we play the confused card. Go all wide-eyed. Say something odd. Maybe you're looking for the freestyle painting class or the quilting circle or something. Works every time."

Herman coughed a few times, earning a censorious look from Eunice. "If you keep coughing, maybe you should stay outside."

"I'm okay," Herman assured. "Still, I need to point out that not all of us have a reputation for doing daffy things." His hand rested on his own chest before he continued with a twinkle in his eye, "Only the staff knows who the jokers and mischief-makers are…" He paused to move his head the tiniest bit so his gaze landed on Gus and Eunice. "As long as we stay clear of any staff members, we should be good."

A few of the sleuths chuckled but silenced their laughter as voices came closer, along with the staticky crackle of a shoulder-mounted radio. Scaffolding and plastic drop cloths decorated the hallway. A bright white ceiling bore witness to painting in progress. Not knowing where to hide, the sleuths took refuge under scaffolding draped with a paint-splattered drop cloth. The 8x3 foot space provided the bare minimum of hiding space for six sleuths. Even at that, elbows were sticking into soft midriffs other than their own. Personal bubbles burst with the enforced closeness and breaths were held until the voices grew more distant.

"Whoa," Jake whispered. "Too close. Let's get a move on. Hanging out here just makes us look guilty. We shouldn't go in a pack because if we get apprehended, we all get booted out at once. Maybe in twos. That way we can distract, allowing another team to get closer. I'll take Hannah as my partner."

Hannah cut her eyes in Jake's direction and shifted her feet to shuffle closer to her partner. The selection took no one by surprise since Jake had set his sights on the newest sleuth. He got over his initial reluctance to accept Hannah into the group due to the fact she may have embellished a few facts of her past, just as he had. Instead of a bomber pilot, he served as a cargo pilot in the service. Not as sexy but still important.

They ducked out from under the scaffolding and headed down the hall. Gus nudged Eunice. "We should go next to provide a distraction. Those two will definitely need it."

As the last two remaining under the scaffolding, Lola waved her hand in front of her nose. "We need to get going or I might get a headache from the paint fumes."

"Give it time," Herman said and pulled his phone out of his pocket and checked it. "Good. I have over fifty percent power. We might be able to get some photos of the explosion site if we're lucky."

"Hey! Stop!" A masculine voice called out in the distance and firefighters in boot-clad feet dashed by the new construction area.

Herman caught his wife's attention. "Aren't you glad you waited under the scaffolding?"

"Oh, I guess…" Lola acknowledged with a sigh, as she reached out to lift the drop cloth. "We have to move *now*. We only have a small window of opportunity."

"You're right." Herman leaned forward, taking the plastic from her hand and lifting it high to enable a clean exit with her cane. The two of them crept down the hall, straining to make out sounds over the obnoxious alarm blare. Then it stopped, forcing them both to halt and stare at each other. The ensuing silence covered them like a blanket. An outraged shriek shredded the stillness and pinpointed Eunice's location.

"Let me go! I need to get to the trivia contest! You must be working for the other side. How much did they pay you?"

"Ma'am, ma'am! It's not safe for you to be in here," a strained baritone insisted. "Sir, could you help me get your wife out of here?"

It sounded like a plea for assistance from Gus. They both leaned forward to catch what Gus might say. "She's not my wife! No, siree! I wouldn't have her on a bet."

"Wretch!" Eunice shouted and then an audible *thump* followed.

Lola hissed. "I think she hit him."

"She hit someone," Herman replied and then snorted. "Gus should have come up with a better plan. He'll be in hot water for days. I don't envy him."

More protests and the sound of a scuffle ensued. Despite their desire to peek, Herman and Lola stayed in place until they heard the front doors swing open. "Go, Herman! Go get those photos. I'll keep our firefighters distracted."

Giving his wife an uncertain glance, he erupted into an awkward jog. His long legs carried him to where a wall and the door to the administration offices used to reside. A few wires dangled from the hole in the ceiling. Blackened acoustical ceiling tile surrounded a ragged patch of blue sky. The blast carved a hole into the flooring. Herman pulled out his phone, snapping pictures madly, knowing any minute he'd be stopped. In one corner of the room a leather couch remained covered in broken acoustical tile, drywall chunks, and glass shards, but was still in one piece. Papers littered the scene, possibly from the mangled metal cabinet in the corner, wadded like a discarded note.

Interestingly, along with the couch, a few feet of carpet remained, but not much else. A pair of men's black oxfords stood next to the wall. Herman stopped taking photos and gulped. In an age where no one ever bothered to shine their shoes anymore, these had to be Ron's. Only a former soldier who could have been dropped for push-ups during basic training for not having a shine on his shoes would care enough to keep a heavy polish on them.

Shaken by the possibility of what the shoes meant, Herman stood silently, reflecting that less than an hour ago he vowed to talk to the new director and maybe even find out the secret behind his scar. He audibly exhaled, knowing now he'd never discover the story.

In the background, he could hear his wife speaking. "Were you Mister October on last year's calendar? You look like an autumn type of guy. Built like a maple. With that fiery hair, you'd be a red maple."

"No, ma'am. Our department doesn't believe in objectifying firefighters for money," a man replied in an amused tone.

"What a pity." Lola paused, obviously lost without the calendar as a subject. Herman centered the focus on the shoes and snapped a photo. In a way, it summed up Ron—a former serviceman who never forgot the rules service had taught him. Be prompt. Be ready. Be aware. Why hadn't he noticed something wasn't as it should be?

Despondent, Herman lurched out of the room, making sure to smear any footprints he might have made, and then went to rescue his wife, who'd managed to find another topic. Lola smiled up at the tall fireman and asked, "Are you planning a pancake breakfast soon?"

Chapter Five

L ARGE WHITE TENTS dotted the front lawn of Greener Pastures. Despite the unusually warm weather, staff still worried about the welfare of the residents standing outside so long in the bright sun. At least the tents provided shade and possibly a sense of safety. Housekeeping and maintenance had also set up tables and folding chairs inside the tents. The chairs and tables normally reserved for special events carried with them a dusty, unused odor that, hopefully, the breeze would blow away.

Oversized orange thermoses of tea and coffee sat on a rectangular table along with several sleeves of disposable cups. Residents cued up for liquid refreshment as a bulky news van bumped into the parking lot. Someone, possibly staff, had leaked the news of the explosion. The van squealed to a stop, allowing a well-coiffed woman holding a portable mic to slip out. A chunky, bearded man exited from the other side and reached in for a television camera. The van continued on to park near the edge of the grass.

The reporter strode to a couple of uniformed employees standing outside the tent. Trotting behind her, the cameraman fiddled with the camera before hoisting it to his shoulder with a grunt. Another man showed up with a portable sound boom as the reporter smiled and arranged her body position for the most flattering angle. When the cameraman said *go*, she sprang into action. The reporter spoke into her microphone. "We're here on location. Hundreds of grandparents are forced to stand outside in the elements. What's going on?"

An aide who had the microphone shoved into her face blinked, then inhaled hard, which probably sounded like a sucking drain with the microphone. "It's not *that* bad outside. The weather is much better than it usually is this time of year. Not everyone here is a grandparent, either."

"All the same," the reporter continued, gesturing behind her to the tent where residents sat at tables chatting, "these elderly citizens are suffering, possibly in danger. Tell us what happened?"

The aide jerked her head, staring at someone behind the reporter team. "Ah," she sucked in her cheeks. "I have to get back to work."

She wandered off-camera with another aide following her. Not discouraged, the reporter approached residents, who had no clue what happened. A few complained about the disruption of their day. One senior, wanting his fifteen minutes of fame, began elaborating on the state of the nation and how people didn't respect their elders and no one made decent movies anymore.

As soon as the news went live, concerned adult children trickled in to haul their grandparents or parents to a safer location, with Gus's family being one of them. Daniel, the son, arrived in a hybrid auto and worked his way through the crowd until he located his father. The slight man with a receding hairline resembled his father only in the hair department. Unlike Gus, he willingly wore glasses, along with a furrowed brow and expression that announced he expected trouble from his dad.

Spotting his father, he maneuvered his way through the clumps of chattering seniors to the table where Gus sat with his friends. Slowing his pace as he approached his son's table, Daniel's shoulders tensed. He pushed out the words, "I'm here to take you home."

Gus glanced up from his seated position at the table and blinked. "Do I know you?"

Unsure, Daniel glanced at the woman at his father's side, who glared at him. "Is he okay?"

"He's fine," Eunice assured with a firm nod. "Much sharper than younger folks. He's playing with you. Since you seldom visit, he's acting like he doesn't recognize you."

"Oh. Come on, Dad! You know you'd be better off at our house," Daniel insisted, placing a hand on his father's shoulder.

Gus firmed his lips and shook his head. "First, you couldn't wait to put me here, and now you want me to leave. Makes no sense."

Daniel attempted a smile but failed at it, as his lips returned to their former downward position. "I want you to be safe. Comfortable. I already talked to your unit's administrator. She's okay with your leaving."

This earned a snort from Eunice. "She'd like us all to leave. Less work."

A cheer interrupted the conversation. They turned to see what had caused the commotion. Grinning employees scrambled out of the center's van, carrying bulging bags stenciled with the name of a local chicken place. Three rectangular tables pushed end to end served as an impromptu dietary area as the employees donned gloves and portioned out food onto the paper plates. Residents familiar with the process hurried to line up. Gus shook off his son's hand. "I need to get in line before they run out of white meat."

His actions suited his words as he squeezed in behind Eunice, who'd immediately hustled into line as soon as it formed. A little grumbling erupted at Gus's line-jumping maneuver, but not much else. Not willing to give up, Daniel followed his father. "Why won't you come with me?"

"I got friends here. That's what *you* wanted for me. It's safe enough. We'll be in the building before nightfall." He turned his face away and addressed the dietary employee. "Eunice kept my place for me."

The worker nodded at Gus but continued to unpack food. Well aware he'd failed at his mission, Daniel's shoulders drooped. "Do what you want. You always do anyhow."

Gus reached out a hand to catch his son's arm. "I do appreciate you coming to check on me. If you ever want to visit when the center isn't on the news, I'd be open to it."

"You got it," Daniel said and embraced Gus, adding in a low voice, "Call me if you need anything."

"I will," Gus promised.

He watched his son exit the tent before whispering to Eunice, "The Sleuths almost lost their most valuable member."

"Ha! You?" Her eyes narrowed and she smirked. "I thought *I* was the most valuable one."

The line moved forward and they shuffled with it, still conversing. "You are to me, but in this case, I know about explosives."

"I see your point," she agreed as she accepted a plate loaded with fried chicken, a biscuit, mashed potatoes, and gravy. "What? No coleslaw?"

The dietary worker pointed to a side table stacked high with distinctive red and white containers. "Over there."

Eunice and Gus picked up their slaw and condiments and headed toward the round table where the other sleuths waited. As soon as they settled and bit into their chicken, Herman spoke. "Ron's car is gone."

If his vehicle had vanished, perhaps he went with it, which was much better than the alternative. The possibility eased his mind. Ron may not have been at the center too long, but he had endeared himself to most of the residents. The previous director never bothered coming out of her office, let alone saying hello to the folks responsible for her salary.

Gus blinked. "He's okay, right?"

Busy chewing, Herman held up a finger to forestall answering immediately. Jake waved his half-eaten chicken leg and said, "I heard the man never even arrived this morning. What a pity. We could use some solid leadership today."

The news caused Herman to choke on his food, resulting in Lola slapping him on the back. He swallowed and then reached for his drink, taking a large gulp. "I'm all right," he managed in a choked whisper, and then cleared his throat before continuing in a normal tone, "We saw him this morning. We talked to him." Herman shot Gus a meaningful look. "Remember, you were there."

"I'm not so sure." Gus's hand slipped up to his head. "I do remember being on the ground and you hovering over me like an oversized vulture, but everything else is a blur."

Oh, this isn't good, Herman mused to himself. Most days he considered himself as coherent as anyone else and more so than many. Lately, without the excitement of cold cases, every day resembled the one before it. He and Lola woke up, got dressed, listened to the news, and went to breakfast. After breakfast, she sometimes had a salon appointment. On Wednesdays, Lola played

32

backgammon with friends. Thursday, she helped at the center's library. During these times, Herman usually kept Gus company. Before Hannah moved in, Jake used to join them.

If Gus couldn't confirm seeing Ron, had the man actually shown up? For his sake, Herman hoped the man took an out-of-town trip to explain his absence in a time of crisis. Not too long ago, he read an article in a psychology magazine about an experiment with false memories. College students utilized as guinea pigs listened to stories about their childhood.

Some of the stories were intentionally false. Not only did many of the students have a hard time pinpointing the fake story, but others insisted they actually happened, too. Even the very young had a hard time deciding what was real and what wasn't. Had he seen Ron this morning or was he thinking of another morning? If only he could confirm the encounter. At the present time, Gus's memory presented no help. The only other individual who could collaborate his story happened to be missing.

What sense went first? Some of the residents at the facility remarked that nothing tasted as good as it once did. Others declared it was the sense of smell that lessened as they aged. Many of the residents practically bathed in cologne—a few more would benefit from doing so. Occasionally, laughter or a knowing look occurred when a sleuth couldn't quite remember the word they wanted. A parking lot became a place where you left your car, or a kitchen was a place where you cooked. They'd tease each other, calling it a *senior moment*. While he did have a few of those, there had never been an entire morning's worth. His stomach made an uneasy somersault caused by something more than the fast-food chicken.

Chapter Six

THE SUN SLID from its apex above the center and started its westward descent as the firefighters packed up to leave. The rumble of vehicles leaving the parking lot drowned out any other sounds. With lunch finished, most of the residents still sat around the tables. One enterprising individual must have exercised some forethought and exited with a pack or two of cards since a canasta foursome formed at one table. Others napped with their heads on the table, while a handful peered at their phones.

A few actually used the phones for their intended purpose, which anyone could deduce by the overloud conversations. No wonder the sleuths chose to leave the tent and the heavy fried chicken aroma. Just a few steps away from the tent, they milled on the edge of the parking lot, waiting for something to happen.

A group of Greener Pastures department heads huddled near the front door engaged in an animated conversation that included a great deal of hand waving. The former playful breeze grew chilly as clouds chased across the sky. Shadows fell on the tents and residents. The impromptu picnic adventure lost its charm as boredom took a seat and showed no evidence of leaving any time soon.

Eunice pointed to the group deep in discussion. "They'd better be deciding to let us back into our apartments that we're paying plenty for." She shifted her weight from foot to foot. "Some of us need to go to the bathroom."

"Well," Gus gestured to the pink portable restroom pod placed on the property for construction workers. "There's always the porta-potty."

"Nope." She gave a dismissive sniff. "I have standards. I'm sure I'm not the only one who sucked down too much tea, thinking we'd be back inside a long time ago."

Overhearing the conversation, Hannah chimed in as she strolled closer with Jake. "I hear ya. Makes me wonder what's going on inside. Right now, they should be thinking about patching the hole in the roof with the way the clouds are building." She tilted her face upward toward the sky. "It might not be right away, but we'll have rain in under twenty-four hours."

Eunice gave her a slow once-over and then asked, "Who made you a meteorologist?"

Even though Eunice's acerbic tongue tended to be more of a fact than a rarity, Gus still poked her shoulder with a single finger. "Be nice." He pivoted to address Hannah. "She didn't mean it."

The proxy apology resulted in a harrumph and Eunice folding her arms, demonstrating she very much *did* mean it.

"It's okay," Hannah replied. "I studied meteorology in college. Even so, you don't have to take a course to know the darker clouds are rain clouds. They can only hold on to the rain for so long. The clouds have a limit to the amount they can carry."

Eunice chose that moment for a loud, exaggerated yawn.

Car doors slammed close by, causing a brief interruption in the budding spat between the two.

Lance's receding hairline and face popped up above the sedan, and he waved at the sleuths, hurrying to the other side to open the car door for Marcy, the dark-haired woman who had founded the Senior Sleuths. Her exit from the vehicle took longer as Marcy eased from the car and retrieved her cane. Even though she'd been deemed well enough to return to work, Marcy wouldn't be chasing down any criminals on foot.

Lance wrapped an arm around Marcy as the two maneuvered their way through a throng of residents who recognized the former resident and called her by name.

"Look at them," Eunice grumbled. "They act like they have some hold on our Marcy."

Most of the sleuths treated Eunice's statements as being a grand summation of the situation. Perhaps she expected an answer, but what she really wanted was a fight. As a newbie, Hannah didn't know this—yet.

"They're just being friendly."

"Ha!" Eunice's face puckered as if she'd bitten into an unripe persimmon. "Marcy might be friendly, I'll give you that. As for the residents, they're just trying to talk to her to make themselves feel important."

"So? What's wrong with that? I imagine your association with the detective makes you feel important, too."

A kind person might use the word *slender* to refer to Eunice. Another might go with *wiry*. Still others referred to her as *scrawny*, which she was—until her indignation caused her to swell up like a pufferfish. As pufferfish go, she reached her full puffy, indignant potential by the time Marcy approached the sleuths.

"Hey, y'all! I got here as fast as I could to get the 10-43."

Eunice turned to Hannah and explained with a superior air, "10-43 means information."

"I know what it means," Hannah snapped. "I have my own police scanner along with a printed list of the codes."

"Ah," Jake interrupted with a nod to the recently arrived detectives. "It's great to see you. Maybe you can see what you can do about getting us back into our units. We've all had a bit too much together time and could do with some alone time."

Lance saluted with two fingers. "I'll see what I can do," he assured, heading off to where the department heads stood talking with the fire marshall.

"Just a minute." Herman retrieved a nearby folded chair for Marcy. "Here ya go."

"Thank you." She acknowledged his gallantry with a nod. "To tell the truth, I sit all day at work. I don't mind standing for a change. I want to know what happened."

All six sleuths started speaking at once, often speaking over each other and creating a jumble of sound.

"Trivia game."

"Loud alarm."

"Herded out like cattle."

"High explosives smoke."

Marcy addressed the last phrase. "What makes you think it was high explosives smoke?"

All the sleuths focused on Gus, who scratched his head and knitted his brows together. "I used to be the bomb guy in the service. Not the person who makes the bomb, but the one who disarmed them. I got to know the type of smoke—usually up close. Dirty gray smoke equals an intentional explosion. Possibly C-4."

"Interesting," Marcy replied and pulled out her phone, which she used to take notes. Her fingers scurried across the keyboard. Without looking up, she addressed Gus. "You're certain it wasn't dirty *white* smoke. That could result from a hot fire that has some resistance."

Some of the certainty slid from Gus's face, but Herman answered. "I saw the smoke. It was a dirty gray. Besides, I photographed the area where the explosion happened. Sure, some things were blown to smithereens, but other stuff like the sofa looked okay. We're talking explosion, not fire."

Marcy glanced up from her phone and arched an eyebrow. "I'm not even going to ask what you were doing inside. Could you send me the pictures?"

"You got it," Herman replied.

Marcy continued, "Anything else unusual happen?"

The sleuths exchanged glances, possibly trying to define *unusual*. Gus volunteered with a grin, "They brought us some fast-food chicken. They've never done that before. A little greasy but still good."

"Okay," Marcy acknowledged his remark and then prompted the rest of the sleuths. "Anything you noticed might help. Technically, this is the fire department's case. If explosions are proven, then the ATF guys might show." Her nose crinkled as she said ATF. Most local law enforcement officers preferred to handle their own situations as opposed to having out-of-towners show up and start giving orders.

Lola coughed, gaining attention, and then cleared her throat. "I don't have anything to say. Just wish I had some throat lozenges. I will say the staff got us all out of the place in a hurry."

"Not all of us," Herman added in a low, soft voice.

Marcy leaned on her cane as she pivoted to face Herman. "What do you mean? Who's missing?"

He took an audible breath before speaking. "Ron, the director, is missing. His office is where the explosion happened. I didn't want to say anything because no one else seems to remember seeing him today, but I distinctly remember talking to him only minutes before everything blew up."

A few gasps sounded and then light chatter erupted as Marcy tapped her temple. Finally, she said, "Did you mention this to anyone?"

"No." Herman shoved his hands into his pockets and dropped his gaze as he spoke. "I didn't want to. I'd just be another confused senior. I asked Gus, but the explosion knocked him to the ground and rattled his memory. If only there was a way, I could prove Ron walked into that building today."

Questions and suggestions flew about as the sleuths pondered the situation. Jake pointed in the direction of the front doors. "We could fingerprint the door handle for Ron's fingerprints." As soon as he said it, he groaned and held up his hand. "Yes, I know. Don't say anything. I realize about a gazillion people touched that door today."

"The receptionist," Lola suggested with bright eyes and an eager expression. She moved closer to her hubby and patted his arm. "I have faith. If Herman said he saw Ron today, then he did."

"*You* might have faith in Herman," Eunice said. A collective inhale happened, waiting to hear what Eunice might say next. "But I have no faith in that receptionist noticing a bald eagle landing on her desk the way she's always playing games on her phone. She thinks if she keeps the phone in her lap no one will know."

Gus chuckled. "You got that right. If it wasn't for the camera on the front door, I could waltz right past her with no one the wiser." Perhaps feeling the scrutiny of his associates, Gus muttered, "What?"

"Cameras," Marcy crooned the word. "I think I'll go suggest we need to have a peek at the video feed."

They watched as Marcy made slow progress across the lawn toward the group that now included Lance.

Eunice sighed loudly. "I only hope she's more effective than Lance."

Chapter Seven

METALLIC CLANKING AND voices drifted from the center's central kitchen that comprised the fourth wall of the dining area. The sleuths crowded around their usual table in the well-lit dining room. Several residents moved by the open double doors, peeking in to decide if supper might be a possibility after their long day spent outside. Gus gestured for them to come in and yelled, "Supper's almost ready!"

"What is it?" Eunice grumbled. "I heard we were having soup and sandwiches. What happened to our blueberry muffins and chocolate cake?"

Hannah glanced up from her crossword puzzle, her pen poised over a few empty blocks. "These things take time. Surely, you've noticed that as soon as the dietary staff finishes one meal, they start another. There's no downtime to stand around outside."

Aware of the tension between the two before the fire marshall gave the all-clear to enter the building, with the exception of the administration area, the other sleuths watched with interest, possibly wondering if the two would come to blows and should they take cover or try to prevent it?

Eunice's head jerked at the comment and turned to stare at the dietary employees rushing about stocking the drink counter. "I have to say…"

While it probably didn't happen, the sleuths would have sworn in retrospect that everything stopped—all the action, all the chatter—waiting on Eunice's next word.

Her eyes lit up as she said, "…you're right. I never took into account how long it took to fix a meal for residents and staff."

Rather than glory at the moment and obviously being unaware of the rarity of Eunice agreeing with anyone, Hannah settled for a slight nod of acknowledgment and returned to her puzzle. Several audible exhales sounded around the table, proving more than one had held their breath.

Anxious to fill in the silence with mindless, inoffensive chatter, both Jake and Lola talked at the same time. Jake tried to address Herman, who stared at his cell phone.

"What do you think about the upcoming Texas hold 'em tournament? Going to enter?"

Lola's lips tipped up as she asked the table occupants, "Did anyone see that murder mystery last night about the lone house on the cape? The leading man certainly possessed brooding good looks." She paused for a breath and before anyone replied she said, "Jake, I'd be interested in the tournament. Got any flyers on it?"

Jake shook his head. "I meant to copy some when the alarm sounded. I'll get you one later today."

"Thanks." She winked. "I can use the change in routine."

Catching part of the conversation, Herman shot his bride an aggrieved look and then muttered, "Brooding good looks. Brooding good looks don't solve mysteries." He held out his phone to Lola. "Take a look at this. What's wrong with those shoes?"

The phone displayed the edge of the leather couch covered in debris and a pair of shiny, black dress shoes next to the wall. "Ah,"

Lola sucked in her lips as she continued to stare and then asked, "What should I be looking for? The shoes appear okay to me."

"Exactly." Herman agreed and thumped the table. "They aren't even dusty."

"Lemme see…" Gus stretched out his hand for the phone, which Lola gave up. He held the phone up close and then stretched out his arm to hold it at a distance. "Not seeing it."

Not speaking, Herman pushed out from the table and moved to where Gus sat and peered over his shoulder. "That's the screensaver. Here, let me fix it."

After he adjusted the phone, he handed it back to his friend. "Try it now."

Gus once again employed the closeup and distant method by moving the phone closer to his face and then extending his arm. "Hmm," he said and sniffed. "I'm shocked. Hard to believe."

The severity of his tone stopped Hannah from finishing her crossword and had Jake leaning forward to peek at the image. "Here. Let me see."

The cellphone slid across the table to Jake's outstretched hand. Just as sensitive to being perceived as old, Jake seldom wore his readers unless he was in his own room. He blinked at the image and frowned. "Okay. It's a pair of shoes. Black oxfords. What's so surprising about that?"

"Seriously?" Herman said.

Gus moved his head side to side, making a clicking sound with his tongue.

"What?" Jake demanded in a tad louder voice. "What should I have seen that the two of you believe is so obvious?"

The noise in the dining room picked up as more residents entered, talking while finding their seats. Dietary aides, carrying loaded beverage trays, delivered drinks.

Often when things got noisy, Gus resorted to shouting. "Look at that shine! Patent leather shoes. I'd put money on it. Only cheaters wear patent leather. Remember the hours we spent lighting shoe polish, spitting into it, and dabbing nylons into the goo?"

"Disgusting!" a woman at a nearby table offered.

Since on a normal day nothing happened at the home, residents kept a close listen for anything out of the ordinary that could be spun into a decent story. No one knew this better than Eunice, who elbowed her boyfriend. "Keep it down."

Gus leaned forward and lowered his voice. "You noticed patent leather, didn't you, Herman?"

Herman's brow furrowed as he contemplated his answer. "My phone has a few years on it. So, it's not the most up to date. Some folks might be able to make some of those videos they put on social media with it, but I am just a point-and-shoot type of guy. So, even my still pictures aren't outstanding. It would be hard to say if the shoes were plain old leather or patent leather. The important thing is they are placed against the wall without a speck of dust on them. It had to be on purpose. Why? Especially since, with the exception of myself, no one claims to have seen Ron today."

This resulted in some literal head-scratching while Gus settled for rubbing his bald dome. "What about the cameras?"

"Nothing yet," Herman answered with a sigh. "I have every confidence that Lance will get back to us as soon as he finds out."

A few "absolutely" and one "you betcha" confirmed Lance's trustworthiness.

"The thing is," Lola started, "what message are the shoes? Is it to demonstrate Ron *did* visit his office this morning? It's hard to imagine him running around without his shoes. No one mentioned blood, which means Ron escaped from getting hurt. That in itself is remarkable. It brings me back to the shoes. Why leave the shoes?"

"What if…" Eunice held up one finger for attention. "…he took off his shoes when entering his office. Maybe they pinched. It would be a great way to keep them looking shiny. We can't find Ron because someone took him."

No one laughed off the idea of Ron being kidnapped. After all, it wasn't as ludicrous an idea as a bomb exploding in the administration office, and that actually did happen. Herman reached for his phone and pocketed it. "I really should have inspected the shoes. All we can do now is wait to hear Lance's results from the cameras. We'll have to wait for a ransom demand, if it comes."

"If…" Lola echoed the word, her penciled-in, dark brows met in a deep V composed of wrinkles and creased foundation makeup.

The men closed their eyes for a moment. Jake opened his eyes first. "Sometimes, it isn't about money, but I hope it's about money this time."

Chapter Eight

THE SENIOR SLEUTHS cast backward glances at the empty corridor as they slipped into Herman and Lola's standard suite. The unit consisted of a modest open area that served the dual purpose of the dining room and living room. Closed doors led to the single bedroom and another to the bathroom. A splash of colorful throw pillows, with one that spelled out in sequins *What Happens in Vegas, Stays in Vegas*, enlivened the beige sofa. The sofa remained as one of the few pieces of furniture left from Herman's bachelor apartment. A jar candle burning on the coffee table added a cozy touch and scented the air with pine.

Chatter erupted and mingled with the sound of popcorn popping in the microwave. As the sleuths took their seats for the emergency meeting, Lola and Herman bustled around in their pocket-sized kitchen, often bumping into one another as they poured coffee into mugs and arranged plastic bowls on the counter. A beep signaled the popcorn had finished its cycle. Lola opened the microwave door and reached for the steaming bag to empty its contents into the waiting bowls. She remarked as she did so, "I may not be much of a cook, but I can do popcorn."

Her husband, Herman, patted her on the back. "No one does popcorn quite like you, honey."

"Uh-huh," she murmured in reply. Next to the popcorn, she

added a stack of shocking pink paper napkins and then announced to the group, "Grub's ready. Come and get it."

This resulted in a flurry of activity as even more people wedged themselves into the minuscule kitchen to doctor their decaf coffee by adding sugar or cream or in Gus's case, adding a little coffee to his sugar and cream. Jake pulled out a silver hip flask with a grin saying, "It's five o'clock somewhere." He added some of the contents to his cup.

With their refreshments in hand, they returned to their claimed chairs. Herman helped his wife, who avoided using her cane in the tiny apartment, to her spot and then returned to the kitchen to claim their refreshments before taking his place. Since Jake called the meeting, he sat at the head of the table.

Even though no actual leader existed, Jake stood and cleared his throat. This action resulted in Eunice elbowing Gus as she groused in an audible whisper, "This had better be worth my time. I happened to be winning at pool. Had those two crones from E Wing almost crying. I have to say, Ron was a real stand-up guy getting us a billiards table and all."

Realizing that everyone had swiveled to pay attention to Eunice, Jake cleared his throat and slammed his hand on the plastic craft table, not making much noise but knocking over his drink.

"Oh!" Hannah yelped as she pushed away from the table to avoid the flow of coffee. A scurry of activity erupted as napkins blotted up the liquid. Hannah reseated herself, but a bit farther from the table.

Jake sighed, and aware that he'd finally gained everyone's attention, spoke. "I called you all in here because I have a real clue." He bobbed his head in affirmation at the bug-eyed and open-mouthed looks.

"You found a possible suspect?" Herman furrowed his brow, shook his head, and shared a look with his wife.

"Not a suspect, per se…" Jake started. He opened his mouth to explain, closed it, and started again. "It's more like motivation."

Hannah waved her hand for attention, earning some curious glances from the other sleuths who probably thought Jake could have blabbed everything to her if only for bragging rights. "What would that be?"

"Well," Jake rocked back on his heels and puffed out his chest as he spoke. "I happened to overhear some pretty juicy stuff earlier."

A tidbit of possible evidence tantalized as Jake grinned at the group. Most acted interested, but Eunice placed her hands on the table and pushed up. "I don't have all day. Got things to do. If you had actual information, you would have said something by now. If I hurry, I might get back to the pool table while my two plump chickens are still there, ripe for the plucking."

Lola rolled her eyes and snorted. "For their sake, I hope they're gone. Isn't gambling against Greener Pastures' rules?"

"It's only gambling if you lose," Eunice smirked. "Otherwise, it's just another source of revenue."

Red-faced, and possibly aware he'd lost control of the conversation, Jake gripped the table and yelled, "Would you two just give it up?"

Both women turned and glared at Jake.

"Okay," he began again. "Someone is siphoning money from Greener Pastures."

The announcement startled the sleuths, who voiced questions in a rapid-fire manner, mostly repeating the same inquiry.

"Who is it?"

"How do you know?"

Jake held up his hand with palm presented to hold the questions. Getting the hint, the sleuths quit talking and turned expectant faces his way.

"As you know, my niece, Katie, works in accounting."

"We know," Gus interjected with a grin. "She's always willing to let us make copies as long as we don't overdo it."

Jake held up one finger. "I know you know Katie works here. However, it's pertinent."

The squeak of cartwheels outside the door silenced Jake as they all turned to stare at the door. A knock sounded down the hall as opposed to Herman and Lola's door, which caused the focus to swing back to Jake—his cue to continue.

"I happened to be in the office, making copies of the flyers for the Texas hold 'em tournament."

"Tournament?" Eunice's voice swung up in surprise. "When is it? Is there a money prize?"

Gus, who sat beside his excited girlfriend, swiveled to face her and patted her arm. "Jake mentioned it at supper. Don't worry, sweetheart. Right now, we need to concentrate on the case." He gestured to Jake. "Go on."

Upset at the interruptions, but not surprised, Jake sniffed and surveyed the group to be certain no other outbursts were forthcoming. Satisfied, he started again, but spoke a bit faster than usual. "Katie was on her cell, talking in a whisper. I knew then something was up. So, I moved a little closer."

"Go on," Gus motioned for him to continue.

"Since she had her back to me, she didn't notice me moving

closer. I heard her mention she was conducting a secret audit to discover where the money was going."

"What money?"

"Secret audit?"

"Who asked for the secret audit?"

"Who was she talking to?"

The questions flew at him fast, making it hard to decide who said what. "Guys, please." He held up both hands. "I was eavesdropping, which meant I couldn't ask questions. I could only hear Katie's side of the conversation. Here's what I *do* know. The center is hemorrhaging money. Enough to cause Katie to do an audit. From what I heard it's been losing money for two months or more. Whoever is funneling money from the home is designating it as pet therapy funds."

"Pet therapy funds?" Lola repeated the words in a louder voice. "Pet. Therapy. Funds." She shuddered, demonstrating either outrage or cold. "They wouldn't even let me keep my little dog, Bear. There's no pet therapy here."

"There are the dancing poodles," Hannah mentioned, "but the woman volunteers her time. There's nothing involving pets if you discount the large fish tank on G Wing."

"Exactly." Jake's eyes shone, and he smoothed his already slick hair with one hand. "I guess that's why Katie thought it peculiar. Couldn't hear what the other person said, though." His lips twisted to one side. "It might explain the reason behind the explosion in Ron's office. Maybe they intended to destroy the records."

In theory, that would make sense if the records existed as physical objects in ledger books or inside file cabinets. "Could be," Jake affirmed but held up one finger, letting them know he hadn't finished. "If so, it must be someone unaware that things are stored on the cloud. Otherwise, Katie couldn't do an audit."

"Who could it be?" Herman threw out the question as rhetorical, not expecting an answer.

Jake dropped his hand to the table and tapped his fingers, waiting for the sleuths to settle. After considering the matter for an entire night, he'd settled on his prime candidate.

"All right, I'll tell you who I like for the crime."

"Wait," Hannah interrupted, earning a sour glance from Jake. "We don't even know there's *been* a crime. I'm not talking about the explosion, but the pet therapy thing."

"There's been a crime," Jake assured with an emphatic nod. He placed his hand over his heart. "My Katie wouldn't be looking if there wasn't an issue. The most likely candidate is the former director. She had access to the funds and knows even less about technology than all of us put together. She'd be a natural to use pet therapy as a cover and think it would work. Besides, I'm not even sure she knew about the cloud. Why did she quit anyhow?"

The Senior Sleuths traded looks and a few lips pursed, demonstrating the hard work of pulling out drawers on mental filing cabinets to select the needed information. The problem was the older a person got, the more information had been tucked away in the cabinet, making the search longer. Referencing tidbits by odd associations worked against easy retrieval, too.

"Anybody remember her name?" Gus asked and then smirked. "Someone who attracted so little attention could probably get away with murder."

Lola held up her beringed hand. "Don't go running off half-cocked and making assumptions." She arched an eyebrow. "Just because some of us have rattled some cages and sparked a few fires…"

Gus pushed back from the table. "Wait a minute. That fire wasn't my fault. The dishtowel landed just a tad too close to the burner. It could have happened to anyone." He placed his hands on his knees in preparation to stand.

Before he could leave, Eunice grabbed his arm. "Don't be a fool. She isn't talking about you in particular, but all of us." She gestured with her right hand to everyone in the room. "We've all engaged in a few shenanigans…" Eunice's gaze lingered on Lola a few seconds longer than anyone else. "…and one or two of us are probably responsible for a *lot* more." She turned back to Gus. "Stay. You know you'll miss out on who said what if you stomp away in a huff."

"Please, stay," Lola added with a smile. "Anyhow, what I meant was just because we are all out solving cold cases and having adventures, we shouldn't suspect someone who has a perfectly bland life. People live ordinary lives all the time without it being a coverup for sinister activity. I heard she wanted to spend more time with her grandchildren. She left suddenly because her daughter was in a bad crash that broke several bones. I think she was intending to leave anyhow, but the need to help her daughter hurried things up. Never heard anyone call her by her first name, but I'm sure we can find some old letterhead with her name on it."

"Maybe the director isn't the culprit," Herman asserted, wiggling in his chair in an effort to locate some lumbar support. He turned toward his wife and inclined his head.

"Ha!" Eunice slapped the table. "I saw that. You have to back your wife on everything."

Herman realized failure to back his new bride wouldn't serve, especially living in such close quarters. Instead, he cleared his throat. "You know, when the police arrest someone, they're not guilty until proven guilty. We could easily come up with three or four people good for embezzlement."

"Like who?" Jake queried from his end of the table. He flipped open a notebook he had brought and clicked his pen, prepared to write.

"Your niece, Katie."

"What!" Jake yelled as he stood, placed his hands on the table, narrowed his eyes at Herman, and pushed the next words through gritted teeth. "Those are fighting words!"

"Don't go all melodramatic on me." Herman sighed and eased back into his seat. "I'm being hypothetical and trying to prove a point. We're all crime drama fans. There's always one or two suspects we don't want to be guilty. They're actually the good guys, unless it turns out they aren't. Anyhow, someone, such as a detective who doesn't know Katie, sees a single parent who struggles to pay the bills and also works in accounting. Most successful embezzlers know how to move the money around."

"Katie would never do that," Jake uttered in a much softer voice. "Go on. Make your point."

Herman shrugged. "That was it. Anyone could appear guilty depending on what angle you look at it. We need to get the facts before anyone *does* start looking at Katie peculiarly."

A murmur of assent rose, along with various sleuths nodding

their mutual agreement. Since Jake called the meeting, he picked up his pen and wrote in his notebook. On one side in dark, block letters he wrote *suspects* and on the other, *motivation*. "Okay. We need to start somewhere. We'll check out the director. We need her name and the name of her daughter. It would be easy enough to check out if a crash actually happened. Every wreck, every divorce, every name change shows up in the local paper. Let's either nail down this suspect or clear her." His somber gaze traveled over the sleuths, and he folded his fingers together as he announced, "Any questions?"

Gus's hand shot up, and he waved it wildly as if he might not be seen.

Giggling erupted, ruining Jake's attempt at being masterful. Leave it to Gus to spoil the moment. "What is it?"

"Ah," Gus started awkwardly, "I noticed no one mentioned anything about Claude."

"Claude who?" Jake asked with irritation roughening his voice.

"You know. The handyman who got fired. I think he got caught stealing. He swore he'd burn the place down when they escorted him off the grounds." Gus pointed to himself. "I may not hear all that well, but since I get the blame for any fires, I tend to pay attention when someone talks about burning things down." His nose crinkled and he smirked. "To tell the truth, he screamed the words as they helped him out the door."

"Well, then." Jake reached for his pen. "We may need to brainstorm a little longer."

Chapter Nine

ARHYTHMIC KNOCKING sounded on the suite door, causing the sleuths to stop talking and throw cautious glances over their shoulders. The knocking came again. Lola held a finger to her lips and then spoke in a loud whisper. "Wait! It's a pattern. A signal."

"What signal?" Herman asked in a low voice, covering his wife's hand resting on the table. "Should we know it?"

"Huh?" Gus spoke, leaning forward, not wanting to miss anything. The knocking stopped, drawing attention to whoever or whatever was on the other side of the door. Gus gulped, causing all to turn in unison to watch the door as if whoever stood on the other side could pass through the locked door. Encounters with aides who didn't respect the privacy of their clients resulted in locked doors, especially during a sleuth meeting. A metallic creak sounded as the doorknob rattled a bit but did not complete its full revolution.

"Herman! Lola!" a familiar female voice called out. "It's us! Marcy and Lance. We need to talk to you, and I have a suspicion the other sleuths are with you, too."

Expelling an audible sigh of relief, Herman pushed up to open the door as the rest of the sleuths broke into excited chatter at the possibility of seeing their favorite detective and her partner. He flung the door open with a wide grin. "Welcome! Come in." He gestured for the couple to enter while backing up a little.

As the two entered, Herman asked, "How did you know the other sleuths were here?"

Lance smirked and said, "Oh, that was easy. The nurse for your wing told me you must be having a party since all your friends showed up, including the firebug."

"Hey!" Gus protested, well aware who the remark encompassed. "Did they say anything else?"

"Let me see…" Lance's eyes slid upward and his lips pursed for a moment, and then he held up one finger as he dropped his gaze to take in the room. "Well, they did ask me to watch for any open flames."

"Don't touch my candle." Lola lurched from her spot at the table and cupped her hands close to her candle.

Gus snorted and his eyes narrowed. "Like I said before, once you do one little thing, no one lets you forget it."

"Yeah," Eunice inserted and patted her sweetie's arm. "Plain persecution. Anyone could have caught those leaves on fire in the courtyard."

"Leaves?" Herman repeated the word as his shaggy brows drew together. "What fire?"

Gus giggled and then shrugged. "Science experiment. Obviously, a magnifying glass will start a fire." He bobbed his head and added, "I put it out, though. No reason to talk about it. I didn't even know the nurses knew about it."

Marcy, who'd eased onto the sofa, cleared her throat, causing Lance to stammer. "My bad. Just joking. The nurse said nothing except that you all were crowded inside. Sorry."

The apology gentled Eunice's belligerent stance, but Gus's expression drooped. "No nurse mentioned me?"

"Not by name," Lance revealed as he took a seat by Marcy. Their hands slid close and then their fingers intertwined by mutual agreement. "I didn't mean to upset anyone."

"I'm good." Gus said, crinkling his nose. "I've had a lot worse things said about me. Even bad jokes played on me. My real question is, why the visit? Not complaining—it just seems unusual."

"True…" Lance agreed, earning an adoring look from Marcy. As if on cue, Marcy withdrew her hand and pressed her hands together in front of her, flashing her ring. "Normally…" she started. Before she could say anything else, Lola moved closer, staring at her left hand.

"Let me see the ring." She reached out to capture Marcy's hand with her own. "Wow!" She arched her brows and landed an approving look on Lance. "Well done. Tell me everything. Did Lance orchestrate a big proposal scene? Did you help pick out the ring?"

Both Eunice and Hannah moved closer, trying to find a place on the sofa to perch, which resulted in Lance giving up his seat to Hannah. He relocated to the table, sitting with the guys as Marcy spun out the tale.

She beamed, placed both hands on her knees, and spoke. "Well, I guess y'all know Lance and I were seeing each other."

A murmur of agreements and head bobs confirmed the announcement. "Anyhow," she continued, "you know I've been riding the desk at work. All I carry to work is my badge. I leave my gun and cuffs at home."

"Must be hard," Lola said, releasing her grasp on Marcy's hand, which resulted in both Eunice and Hannah reaching for her hand to check out the ring.

"Fancy…" Eunice remarked, arching her brows and peering at

Gus.

Marcy wiggled her hand free and stared at the ring. "It's pretty awesome."

"Go on," Lola urged. "I want to hear the whole story."

The former resident simpered and shot a look at her beloved. "Lance did it right. He shows up at work and asks me if we can talk about a particular case. We have a small conference room with a two-way glass that sometimes we use for questioning. When I opened the door, it was the perfect romantic scene."

"Tell us more," Eunice urged, moving closer to elbow Marcy. "Some of us have to live through others' grand romantic gestures."

Placing a hand over her heart, Marcy sighed. "It took my breath away. Instead of the usual ugly furniture and bland room, it had been transformed with a red tablecloth, roses in a crystal vase, two lit red candles, and on the table was—"

Before she could finish, Eunice did. "A magnum of champagne chilling and two wine glasses?"

"Nope," Lance offered from across the room. "No alcohol in the station. It's strictly against the rules."

"Then, what?" Eunice asked. "What else was there? How did you know it was a proposal?"

Marcy giggled. "I'm a detective, after all. What else could it be when there was a shiny pair of handcuffs with a fancy ring resting inside one cuff."

"Ooh! Handcuffs," Lola purred the words and then gave the middle-aged Lance a second look. "Still waters run deep."

"Not that deep," Marcy insisted. "He used the handcuffs because he had a theme."

This resulted in a flurry of feminine giggles. "What would that be?" Hannah asked before someone could.

"Prisoner of love," Marcy admitted, causing the men in the group to groan. "He dropped to one knee and proposed, telling me he was a prisoner of my love."

A chorus of *ahs* announced Lance netted romantic hero in several pairs of eyes. "So," Marcy continued, "I feel like we wouldn't have gotten together if all of you hadn't pushed us together. Somehow, I missed what was staring me directly in the eyes. Whenever I felt something a little more than appreciation for a great partner, I reminded myself he was five years my junior. Besides, I didn't want to lose a good partner."

"Same here," Lance explained with a grin. "Only in my case, I wanted a life partner."

Lance endured several slaps on the back and a trio of perfumed hugs. "We did come here to tell everyone about the proposal, but also to ask if you'd like to be part of the ceremony. It'll be a small one. Something soon since we're getting older every day."

The announcement caused much chatter and questions.

"Have you bought a dress?"

"What colors have you chosen?"

"Who's going to be a bridesmaid?"

Expectant eyes fixed on Marcy. She cleared her throat and explained, "It's a super small wedding. We'll probably just go to the courthouse. We weren't really thinking about having attendants, but if I was, I couldn't pick just one maid of honor. It would have to be *all* of you."

Smiles and titters greeted her announcement while the male senior sleuths raised speculative eyebrows in Lance's direction.

"Same here," he added. "Too many great sleuths to choose from for best man."

"Great! That means we're all in the wedding. We need to start planning," Herman announced, feeling a sense of pride at being asked to be a part of Lance and Marcy's wedding. He puffed out his chest and grinned. He hadn't participated in any sibling weddings and with no adult children, there was none in the offing.

Suggestions flew across the room from practical to far-flung.

"You might be able to use the D Lounge for your reception," Lola suggested. "It would give the other residents a chance to wish you well."

A raspberry sounded and Eunice stuck her tongue out, demonstrating her opinion. "Forget about those hangers-on. It's your wedding. Do something special. Get married in a hot air balloon. People do it all the time."

"We could," Marcy agreed and crinkled her nose as she continued, "but there'd be no room for all of you."

"Forget that!" Eunice declared, willingly giving up on her idea.

"Just as well," Jake said. "I've spent all the time I want in the air. My goal now is to keep my feet on the ground."

"You know," Hannah inserted in a soft voice that forced the others to stop talking just to hear. She pushed her hair back behind one ear as she continued, "There's a little chapel in the woods near my old home. They do what they call elopement packages because the groups are so small. The grounds are beautiful with flowers everywhere. They even have a brick path with the names of the couples married there. A white gazebo serves for an outdoor wedding or a small non-denominational chapel for an indoor wedding. Reasonable prices, too. Three hundred for an indoor or outdoor wedding and they provide the officiant and set up the chairs and stuff. All you have to do is show up."

Marcy inhaled deeply, brought her index finger to her lips, and then dropped it. "We don't want any fuss. With work and all, I don't have time to plan any fancy event."

Pairs of interested sleuth eyes switched between watching Marcy sucking in her lips to Lance's furrowed brow. "Honey," he began, "it doesn't sound too involved if you're interested. I know people plan these things out years in advance. They might not have an opening."

Another audible exhale came from Marcy as she entwined her fingers and dropped her gaze to her engagement ring. "I don't know. Never planned on getting married." She raised her eyes and managed a half-smile. "Maybe when I was really little and they had all those bride dolls looking so much like princesses..." She shrugged her shoulders. "As I got older and started on the force, all thoughts of marriage faded as I witnessed fellow officers' marriages crashing and burning due to the unpredictability of police work. There were missed ball games, children's plays, and birthdays."

Lance stood and made his way to his fiancée, standing behind her and placing his hands lightly on her shoulders. "Those officers married young. They didn't know what they were getting into, but we're not like that. We both know what the job entails. Besides, the only disappointed children we have are Domino the cat, and Bear the dog. Since there will be two of us to care for them, they will think they've won the pet lottery. Why not have a wedding in the woods or whatever it's called?"

"Well," Marcy reached to cover one of her sweetie's hands with her own. "I suppose we could look into it."

"Super!" Eunice announced and clapped her hands together. She turned slightly to make eye contact with all the sleuths. "Hannah can email you the information and the rest of us can make this wedding happen. All we need is a date. With the Senior Sleuths on your side, what could possibly go wrong?"

Chapter Ten

T HE OVERHEAD LIGHT fixture could have doubled for a baseball park floodlight the way it lit up the room and bleached the pastel blue walls to an almost white. It caught the lenses of Hannah's readers as she perched on the sofa and regaled the other female sleuths and Marcy with forgotten wedding traditions. Her brows arched as she crinkled her nose and asked, "How many of you have caught the bridal bouquet?"

"A few times," Marcy admitted and rolled her eyes, "when I was a kid, not more than a teen." She shook her head and grimaced a bit. "Later, once I turned thirty-one, I felt the bride either aimed for me or people expected me to break through all the giggling young females like a linebacker. If I'd known what was coming, I'd have headed for the restroom to avoid it."

"Ah, sweetie…" Lola patted Marcy's hand and pulled a smile from the reluctant bouquet catcher.

Not one to pick up on subtleties, Eunice sat up ramrod straight and pushed out her meager chest as she announced, "I caught the bouquet *every* time. If I was there, it was mine." She gave her head an airy toss as she elaborated. "The other girls, they were pushovers. They didn't want it enough. Rather disappointed that once I got married, I couldn't compete for the bridal flowers anymore."

The image of Eunice flying through the air to catch random

tossed flowers earned a few laughs. Hannah waited for them to die down before adding, "You wouldn't have wanted to catch the bouquet they threw in the Middle Ages when the tradition originally started. Garlic, chives, and dill made up most of it. Since folks didn't believe in bathing back then, having a bunch of folks together for a wedding could be a bit pungent. At least the bride got a little break with her spice bouquet."

"How do you know the garlic wasn't to hide her own smell?" Eunice inquired with a smirk.

"It could be," Hannah admitted, showing no upset at being interrupted.

Herman, Jake, and Gus kept Lance company at the table. Due to the diminutive size of their apartment, all conversations became shared conversations. Jake snorted, "All your old traditions involve women. Are there none for men?" He used a backward-pointing thumb to indicate Lance sitting nearby. "What about him?"

Gus made a mumble of agreement and elbowed Herman. "You agree, right?"

Herman blinked and then sputtered, "Yes, of course."

Before Hannah could speak, Eunice half rose from her seat, waving her index finger. "I have one. The father of the bride has to pay for everything."

"Not a good tradition," Gus groused, frowned, and folded his arms. "Even the most practical, level-headed girl goes half-crazy with dreams of wedding cakes as tall as a person and being driven around in a carriage fit for Cinderella. Don't you have anything better?"

Everyone chuckled at Gus's comment, possibly imagining various bridezillas. Hannah held up her hand, waiting for her audience's attention to return to her, demonstrating her ability to hold children spellbound at library story time. Once the sound dissipated and all eyes returned to her, she spoke. "It used to be only men could give the toasts."

"Sounds about right," Jake added with a twinkle in his eye.

Lola huffed. "I'd expect as much…" She paused to narrow her eyes in Jake's direction before continuing. "…from a man."

This only made Jake smirk more. "How about burying the bourbon? What about that tradition?"

"What?" Hannah pushed her slipping readers up her nose. "I don't know that one. Why don't you tell it?"

"Not sure how good I'll be at it." He shrugged his shoulders. "I'll give it a go. I met this guy from Kentucky. He told me when someone is going to get married, you go to where the wedding will take place and bury a fifth of bourbon. When the wedding happens, the bourbon is dug up and drunk."

Lance sucked in his lips and exhaled. "I guess that's one way to age liquor."

"They did it for luck," Jake explained. "Never heard anyone else talk about this. So, it could be a regional thing."

"Possibly," Hannah agreed as Herman allowed talk to swirl around him. Why hadn't Lance mentioned the cameras? Maybe he did see the film and it contained only the wide lawn and himself and Gus. Being the courteous fellow, Lance might sidestep the entire issue rather than draw attention to Gus's memory lapse.

Hannah launched into another tradition, something about the reasons behind the expression *something old, something new, something borrowed, something blue, and a sixpence in her shoe.*

Mentions of something old representing the bride's past faded as Herman grappled with the elephant in the room. Had he mistaken the day? With the sameness of his current schedule, the days mirrored one another.

A throat clearing nearby broke into his reverie. Lance gave a slight nod and angled his head in the direction of the kitchen. No one needed to tell Herman twice. He stood and carried his cup to the kitchen as if for a refill while the others listened to the importance of blue in the wedding ensemble for luck. Coffee trickled into his cup as Lance joined him, holding up his own cup.

"I could use a refill."

Herman nodded. "Might need to start a new pot." He suited his actions to his words, filling up the carafe with water, dumping out the old grounds, and inserting a new filter and fresh coffee grounds. "Should be done in a jiffy." As he poured the water into the coffeemaker, he casually added, "Find out anything about the cameras?"

"Took you long enough to ask." Lance saluted him with his cup. "I admire your patience. Not sure I could wait as long as you did."

"And?" Herman prompted.

"Cameras were working until the explosion." When it looked like Herman might ask for more details, Lance held up his index finger. "Let me clarify. All the cameras except for the ones on the front door and loading dock."

"What?" Herman lifted his cup to his face for a sip and to hide his disappointment.

"They were turned off."

"That's convenient…" Herman inhaled deeply and lifted his shaggy brows. "Fingerprints?"

"They're checking."

In a few words, Lance managed to convey that they weren't on the case and suspicious camera tampering had occurred. That meant he saw Ron—and was possibly the last person to do so.

Chapter Eleven

HEAVY DARKNESS RESTED beyond the apartment windows of Herman and Lola's unit—not the type that followed late afternoon, hinting at the approaching night and hurrying diurnal creatures to seek out their homes—the solid black that manifests before stars or moonlight manage to pierce it. Usually, it didn't happen before ten-thirty in the summer, but with the season and the daylight savings time change shortening the day, full night could come as early as eight o'clock.

The same lack of light that sent people scurrying inside to places of safety sent out others who took advantage of the shadows. Night insects started their chorus, accompanied by tree frogs, about the same time as Marcy and Lance said their goodbyes to the sleuths. Lola made her way to the window by grabbing onto the furniture as her balance chose to leave her without so much as a warning. She peered out the glass, catching sight of headlights. "There they go. I understand them needing to get home to take care of Bear and Domino. I still wish they'd stayed longer. There's so much I wanted to discuss about the wedding."

"That surprises me…" Herman moved to stand close to his wife and placed an arm around her waist. "It wasn't that long since our marriage. Remember, we had two weddings."

"Who could forget?" Lola cuddled into her husband's half-embrace. "The one for your friends in North Carolina and then the other in Vegas. All this for a woman who never expected to marry." They enjoyed a tender moment while their guests bickered.

Gus placed a fisted hand on one hip and asked in a thin, high tone, "You mean the guys aren't invited?"

"Nope," Eunice announced as her chin went up a notch and her shoulders back. "It's a woman thing." She reached for her purse and shouldered her bag. "Better get going. I need my beauty sleep if I'm going to help Marcy find the perfect dress."

Eunice marched to the door, opened it, and left without a backward glance at her steady beau. If she had, she'd have noticed that Gus's mouth had dropped open. After the door shut, Hannah gathered her things but chose to address Gus before taking her leave. "It may sound like a big deal, but you'd be bored silly. Lots of standing around comparing dresses that pretty much look the same and then leaving the store with nothing to show for it."

"You're not wrong when it comes to the basics. I'm not an ordinary fellow," Gus gleefully said. He pointed back to himself. "Now, when I shopped with my wife, I made a game of it. She might do a slow stroll through the mall searching for sales while I pretended to be a secret agent. Many times, I'd feign an accent and sidle up to a sales clerk with a cryptic phrase like *the penguin howls at midnight. Do you samba*? I'd wait a little and then say, 'Oh sorry, you're not the one.'"

"Oh my," Hannah shook her head and grinned. "Here I thought I was the only one who engaged in role-play. Any other shopping games?"

"Tons," Gus revealed with a wink. "One of my favorites is when

I see someone considering if they should buy an item and I simply saunter over and say, 'Get it. You deserve it.'"

"That made you popular."

"You'd think, but no one ever thanked me. Didn't even get a commission from the store."

Jake, who'd been listening to the entire conversation without saying a word, grunted and mumbled something indecipherable under his breath.

"I heard that," Gus said as he turned around to face his friend.

"Prove it," Jake challenged and lifted his coffee cup to his lips.

"Don't have to. I know it's something best left unsaid." He carried his cup and saucer to the kitchen. "I need to get going, too. Thinking about entering the Texas hold 'em tournament. So, everyone, get ready to lose."

"Ha!" Jake forced out a laugh. "No worries. I'll try not to be too hard on you."

Ignoring the comment, Gus moved to bid his hosts goodbye and left with a simple wave to Hannah. Taking his exit as a cue, Hannah peeked at her wristwatch and then at the door. "I'd better get going." She turned slightly, her rubber-soled shoes squeaking on the tile floor. "Oh, Jake, could you get me a form for the poker tournament?"

He gave her a double look but then said, "Will do."

Since their guests were leaving, Herman and Lola abandoned their place at the window to bid them goodbye. Lola slid into a nearby chair with a heavy sigh. Seeing his wife comfortably situated, Herman moved on to chat with his old pal.

Lola nodded at Hannah. "Everyone is playing Texas hold 'em all of a sudden."

Hannah chose to perch on the edge of the couch, placing her at the same level as her hostess. "I've noticed. The game gained popularity in the 1970s at the Horseshoe Casino in Vegas. Probably most notable for its no-limit games."

"Whoo!" Lola expelled an audible breath. "Whenever I forget you're a librarian, you go and say something like that. What I was trying to point out is the residents around here can be competitive. Eunice in particular."

"Just a little," Hannah snorted. "I noticed that." She tapped her own chest with three fingers. "I've been called a card shark myself a time or two. Don't worry about me. I welcome the competition." Hannah stood, thanked Lola for her hospitality, and left with a bounce in her step.

"Why does everyone think they're Diamond Jim Brady?" Lola stared at the door and pushed up from her seat. This time she reached for her cane and shuffled toward the bedroom.

"She's tired." Herman watched his wife go into the bedroom. He yawned and nodded at his friend. "I'm pretty beat, too. Traumatic day."

"Know what you mean," Jake said. His hand slipped up to rub the back of his neck. "I'll be heading out, too." He took a couple of steps in the direction of the door and then stopped, turning slightly to address his friend. "No reason to go investigating the embezzling. No reason at all. Not our place."

Herman made an indecipherable grunt that could be taken as assent while promising nothing. The door clicked shut. Before locking it, he stared at it, replaying Jake's words. On any other day, his friend would be all about sniffing out a mystery. No doubt the man thought he'd settled any type of sleuthing by telling Herman not to investigate. In some ways, it worked better than waving a red cape in front of an angry bull. Not that he imagined himself as a bull, but more as a bloodhound that happened to pick up a scent. There was no way he could abandon it now.

Chapter Twelve

THE AROMA OF bacon and coffee crowded in the dining room along with the residents. The floral curtains pulled wide allowed patchy sunlight to dance across the faux stone linoleum and the wooden pedestal tables. Chatter along with laughter, especially at the sleuths' table, filled the room. The female sleuths acted especially excited, giggling, and leaning over to whisper in each other's ears.

Gus huffed and caught the attention of Jake and Herman. Once he did, Gus frowned and growled a little. "Look at them, as giddy as school girls. Eunice even put on makeup this morning. Eunice. Makeup. Did you hear what I just said?"

"Who couldn't?" Jake chortled, throwing his head back and drawing attention to their table. A nearby diner shouted, "What's so funny?"

Jake pointed to Gus, which had the resident snorting and turning back to his breakfast. In typical fashion, Herman cleared his throat and said, "Yes, the girls are excited. Lola hummed *Get Me to the Church on Time* while she put on her makeup. It makes sense they're excited. Besides, it couldn't happen to a nicer couple. I wonder if anyone is doing anything for Lance? Do they make a day of having a tux fitting?"

The question stopped the feminine chatter. Lola answered with, "No. Lance is wearing a suit. Most guys have a bachelor party. Some even have a road trip—not feasible though, with the two getting married so soon. That reminds me, we need to check out The Pines for openings." Without waiting for help, Lola pushed out from the table, leaving her half-eaten breakfast, and reached for her cane.

"I'll help, too," Hannah said, rising to her feet and accompanying Lola.

Not a half-minute later, Eunice had finished her breakfast and glanced up, arching her brows. "They need my help, but they're too proud to ask."

Once the women left, Jake rubbed his hands together. "Good. Now we can plan the bachelor party."

"What party?" Herman wondered aloud. Had he missed something? "Didn't we just say there's no time for anything?"

"Nothing *big*," Jake said, blinking twice while lowering his voice. "What kind of guys would we be if we didn't do something for the groom?"

"Yeah," Gus interjected with a giggle. "*I'm* your fun guy."

"Oh, we all know that," Herman concluded with a side glance. His fingers, resting on the table, tapped against the wood, creating a muted rhythm. "We don't have much time, not a lot of money to speak of, and we definitely don't want to do anything that would make Marcy mad. Don't want Lance to start marital life with an angry bride. So, what do you have as far as suggestions?"

With Herman's list of what they didn't have and shouldn't do, Jake melted back in his chair, putting up his hands as if giving up. "I've got nothing."

"Me, either," Herman admitted and pushed away his plate. "I heard one time about guys getting together for a clean bachelor party and all they did was write down marital advice and glue the slips of paper into a scrapbook. We're probably not the guys to give advice. When I heard this tale, it started with *this is the absolute worst thing to do for a bachelor party.*"

"Sounds about right," Jake concluded, reaching for his coffee.

"You guys…" Gus opened and closed his hands resting on the table, and his eyes shone as he spoke. "…have no imagination. There's a *lot* we can do. We can skydive."

"Too expensive," Herman inserted—not to mention dangerous. Marrying Lola made him want to live longer to enjoy their shared lives.

"How about herding cattle?" Gus suggested. "It will put us out of our comfort zone. I saw it in a movie a way back."

"*Way* out of my comfort zone," Jake acknowledged. "Who do we know who has cattle that need to be herded here in the Midwest? Why would they let us do so?"

"Good point." Gus's brow furrowed as he considered the matter. "We need something fast, fun, and cheap."

"Sounds like we're on leave again," Herman said, looking left, then up, and possibly recalling images when they were young GIs out on the town with very little folding money in their pockets.

"Ah, those were the days," Jake murmured with a wistful smile. "Can't say I'm up to visiting the various community centers hosting liberty dances. Knees can't cut a rug the way they used to for hours at a time." He leaned forward and wagged a finger at both Herman and Gus. "Don't any of you mention my less than perfect knees to Hannah."

Herman harrumphed, wondering if his friend assumed Hannah's eyes missed out on the fact that he no longer resembled a twenty-year-old, or even a fifty-year-old for that matter. Dark hair dye could only do so much. Gus, being himself, crinkled his nose and pointed out the obvious. "You don't have to worry about us. It's the women, filling Hannah's ears with your various shenanigans, you have to worry about. I imagine she's already heard it all and still likes you." His face contorted into an expression of distaste. "There's no understanding taste."

Someone laughed at the nearby table, demonstrating that eavesdropping served as a popular pastime. A silver-haired man from the next table wheeled his chair over to the sleuths' table. "Hello, gentlemen! I'm here to solve your problems."

"Hi, Wilson," the three chorused with a decided lack of enthusiasm.

Politeness designated Herman to hear the man out. "What's *your* plan?"

"Leisure Time Fun Park." Wilson grinned. "My grandson owns it and it has everything. Laser tag, mini-golf, arcade games, and a go-kart course. Lots of people book it for birthday parties, business retreats, and such. Why not a bachelor party?"

"Thanks," Herman said and gave the man a polite nod, which should be enough for him to go back to his table. Only, he didn't. Not sure how to wind up the conversation, Herman patted his pockets down and pulled out his phone. "Oh my, it's Lola! Got to go."

Before Herman reached the door, he could hear Gus feigning a message from Eunice. If nothing else, it got them away from the juvenile plan of having a bachelor party at a go-kart park. After all, they were dignified, mature men, and this dignified male needed to do a little sleuthing today.

Chapter Thirteen

F AMILIAR FEMININE LAUGHTER drew Herman to the center lobby decorated with overstuffed chintz loveseats and large potted palms. Morning sunlight highlighted the female sleuths with a broad beam as they peered out the window for their ride. Even though he might give the impression of a besotted swain, Herman made the decision to bid goodbye to his bride one more time and steal a kiss.

Since they were facing the windows, none of them saw or heard him coming, being much too involved in their own conversation. Eunice turned slightly to address her companions. "I need to arrange a bridal luncheon. Do you think I can get the D Wing Community Room or would a restaurant be better?" Before anyone could respond, Eunice continued, "Restaurant, of course. I heard Cook's Table has an excellent barbeque." She gave a dramatic sigh. "So many responsibilities come with being the maid of honor. Who do you think I should invite?"

Lola's head jerked so hard at the comment that a chiropractor visit could figure in her future. "Maid of honor?" she asked in a raspy contralto. The tone caused Herman to take a step back. Thank goodness he'd never merited that particular pitch.

"Oh, you know," Eunice tilted up her chin. "Some things don't need to be said. You just know. Obviously, she doesn't want to hurt *your* feelings." Her eyes slid to Hannah. "She doesn't really know you—so you would never be a choice."

"I didn't expect to be," Hannah offered, showing no emotion, demonstrating what an amazing poker player she'd be. "What I heard was no matron of honor or bridesmaids. It's not a requirement to have *any* attendants. Small wedding, you know? Marcy didn't invite us to go dress shopping because she needs our help, she did it to be kind. Break up the monotony of our week. Let's not make her regret her generous action with your junior high drama."

Lola sniffed, probably feeling lumped in with Eunice. A distraction would smooth over an awkward moment.

"Hello, ladies!" Herman said as he strolled closer to his wife. "I couldn't let this beauty go without another kiss."

"Ugh." Eunice made a gagging sound and turned away as Herman brushed his wife's papery cheek with his lips.

"How sweet," Hannah remarked.

Lola placed her cool fingers on his cheek. "What will you be doing, dear, while I'm gone?"

Before they'd left for breakfast, he'd mentioned his desire to pursue the mystery of the missing Ron and the bigger issue that no one acted alarmed about it. "I'm going to do a little digging on our very own mystery. Not sure why no one is interested in it."

"Oh pshaw." Eunice gestured as if brushing off the remark. "Gus called Lance and told him all about Claude. I wouldn't be surprised if the scoundrel isn't in jail by nightfall." She folded her arms as if that settled the case.

"I'd be interested in hearing how that turns out," he acknowledged with a short nod. "I'm taking a different approach." It was not one he wanted to discuss openly, though. To avoid doing so, his height allowed him to see around the women and into the parking lot. "Is that Marcy driving a mini-van?"

This resulted in all three women rushing to the window.

"Oh, it *is* her!" Hannah said. "We should get going." She shouldered her bag as the other women did likewise. Both Hannah and Eunice pushed out the door, but Lola hesitated, glancing back at her husband. "I'll help when I get back."

"I'll hold you to that," Herman promised and waggled his shaggy brows. He lifted his fingers to his lips and blew her a kiss. His bride motioned catching it with her free hand and then holding her hand to her heart. Herman darted ahead to open the heavy door for her. After he closed the door, he pivoted only to see the receptionist with her head down, staring at something in her lap—probably her phone. A sheepherder could drive a flock through the lobby, complete with a barking border collie and at best, she might mention the smell. The woman might even have some of those wireless earbuds like Gus. Well, he knew one thing—no confirmation whether Ron had arrived yesterday morning would come from that quarter.

Yellow tape stretched across the bombed-out area, along with a hand-lettered sign that instructed people to go down B Wing and turn right to get to the various wings. It was no easy task working through the maze of wings that had grown over the past years. Residents formed walking clubs that used wrist-watch style monitors to count their steps. A few boasted if they walked down every wing, it was the equivalent of a mile and a half. Other residents insisted they walked five miles some days—a claim Herman doubted.

Herman had no intention of using the detour. His real goal was a closer inspection of the destroyed area. So far, no men in suits paraded through the lobby acting both self-important and irritated. Maybe they had gotten what they needed the other day. Blue tarp stapled in place covered the roof hole. As measures go, it wouldn't keep out the autumn storms. A real replacement needed to happen pronto, which would result in roofers inside and out, stomping around, and destroying evidence.

As fellow residents turned to stare at the blocked-off area, Herman moved closer to a still life of waxy fruit and dying flowers. Who picked out this art? Talk about depressing. The couple behind him grumbled about taking the long detour. Herman could duck under the yellow tape if the hall remained empty.

Their image reflected in the picture glass allowed Herman to gauge when the couple was far enough away to sneak under the tape. Since anyone could show up at any time, from ATF agents to the fire marshall, he needed to get in and out as fast as possible. Keeping his eye on the dining doors, Herman hunched under the tape and backed into Ron's office before anyone could see him. The missing wall failed to offer much coverage. He slid back another step and bumped into something.

"Oops," a feminine voice murmured. Herman whirled to see who'd caught him in the act of compromising a crime scene. He'd done it now. Not only would he be censured by Greener Pastures, but he'd also get a talking to from Lance and Marcy—one of those lectures that might include the phrase *I'm so disappointed in you*. Lectures never went down easy but stuck more when the lecturer happened to be significantly younger.

Instead of a uniformed fire official or a suited agent, Katie's startled gaze met his. Why would Jake's niece sneak into Ron's office? Before he could ask, he noticed the patent leather oxfords in her hands. "Why do you have Ron's shoes?"

She inhaled deeply and blinked a few times before answering. She spoke in a rush. "They're not Ron's shoes." She held them closer to her chest as if Herman might try to wrestle them from her.

"They were in Ron's office. It makes sense they'd be Ron's shoes."

She shook her head hard as a tear made its way down her cheek. "Not Ron's shoes. They're patent leather. Ron wouldn't be caught dead in patent leather shoes."

"I would have thought as much." Before he could say anything, Katie continued,

"They're the wrong size, too."

Were they? Herman stared at the shoes, suddenly aware he had no clue what size shoes Ron wore. Knowing someone's shoe size struck him as personal. How well did Katie know Ron? Why steal the shoes that didn't belong to Ron? "How would you know that?"

"Well, ah…" She leaned to peer around Herman. "…I really need to go."

Even though his appearance at the crime scene might compromise evidence, at least he hadn't snatched anything. "Don't you think you should leave the shoes as evidence?"

"No." She inhaled audibly and backhanded a tear. "I bought the shoes as a joke because patent leather was something he'd never wear. Couldn't find his size. I figured once he saw them, he'd know it was me and come stomping over to my office. You know how old school he was. Everything by the book." She took another noisy breath. "All the same, I liked him."

Ron and Katie. He never imagined a budding attraction between the two of them. "*You* left the shoes?"

"I did. They were in a box. The fact that they weren't in a box meant he saw them, or maybe they were blown out of the box. Even though they didn't technically belong to him, they're the only thing I have to remind me of Ron. I'm surprised they didn't take them. On those crime shows, they take everything, including pulling up the carpet. I come in here and the shoes were swept into a corner with the other debris."

Odd they hadn't taken the shoes. Color him unimpressed when it came to the agents' crime scene inspection. Maybe they had a reason not to look too hard. Katie stood clutching the shoes, trembling.

Even though she might be an embezzler, Herman sympathized with the woman. While greed fueled most crimes, many occurred when people failed to make their paycheck stretch to cover basic expenses. Add to that the heartbreak of not knowing what happened to a current love interest. "I'm sure he's okay. He must have lined up the shoes by the wall before…" he paused, not knowing what to add since he had no clue what had occurred. Even if he did mention that her previous gentleman friend may have blown up, it wouldn't help. Crying women terrified him. He never knew what to do to get them to stop.

She hugged the shoes tighter. "That helps. He *did* see the shoes. He knew."

On that note, she slipped around him and vanished down the hall. What *did* he know? Did Ron know Katie helped herself to extra funds? Perhaps Ron dipped into the money, too. He turned slowly, noticing most of the furniture had been pushed against the wall and the debris swept into a pile. The wind teased the tarp, pulling it enough to send down shafts of sunlight every other breeze. There was a good chance housekeeping decided to tidy the place up. Any good agent would have taken photos. There was not much to see, but Herman searched the room, looking for any evidence that Ron knew about the explosive. His jacket still hung in the open closet. Had he been wearing his jacket?

On his desk, a dark red stain stood out on the desk calendar. He leaned over and sniffed it to see if he could pick up the coppery scent of blood. Unfortunately, his sense of smell just happened to be one of the many things that wasn't as good as it once was. "You'd think they would take the blotter. Nothing about this case adds up."

Chapter Fourteen

Herman sat in his favorite leather club chair and brooded. The chair conformed to his body from serious use over the years. The arms and seat cushion, shiny with age, announced its status. Soft instrumental music played in the background. Old songs that he once knew so well now failed to work their magic to stop his brain from spinning.

What if Katie was guilty? Would a guilty person do her own secret audit? No need to if she knew where the money went. Then again, the audit talk could be a smokescreen. Would he be able to do the right thing and turn her over to the authorities, or would he be like one of the popular television cops who allowed a battered woman who killed her abusive husband to vanish into the night? Skimming a few thousand hardly equaled murder. Maybe a deal could be worked out to pay back the purloined money without any jail time.

His frown lines deepened as he mentally spun out the various scenarios that he'd been doing all afternoon. He bypassed lunch, afraid he couldn't face Jake across the dining room table. Instead, he put a bag of popcorn into the microwave for a snack. Usually, Lola prepared the popcorn, insisting the instructions on the bag didn't suit their microwave. Herman settled for pushing the popcorn button and hoping for the best. An acrid aroma hinted that his choice stank—literally.

He inhaled deeply even though he sucked in the smell as he did so. Katie made sense, but Ron? Administrators could make up to six figures, although Greener Pastures directors may not have netted as much. Still, it made no sense. Perhaps Ron had a gambling problem. If so, maybe he had romanced Katie, the accountant, to cover his tracks. The thought of revealing such information to Katie made him groan.

The apartment door opened at the same time that Herman groaned. Lola paused in the doorway and sniffed. "Do I want to know?"

"No." Herman made an effort to get out of his chair without initial success.

"Stay seated. I can get into our apartment on my own. What you *can* do is tell me what put you in such a mood."

He sighed, leaned his head back and gazed at the ceiling, pondering what he should say. "Nothing."

"Ha!" Lola slammed the door and worked her way to the sofa, leaning a bit more on her cane than usual.

"You're tired," Herman exclaimed, pushing out of his chair and hovering by his wife. "Can I get you anything? A drink? A pillow?"

Lola flopped back into the overstuffed sofa and closed her eyes. She spoke with her eyes still closed. "All I want is a straight answer from you. First of all, you're not that good an actor. Besides, I learned to read faces in Vegas. I can tell when a poker player is bluffing and in my real estate career, I could spot the folks insisting they won't take less than a certain amount, but they will. It's obvious to me something is eating away at you. Spit it out."

Herman groaned, sighing heavily. "It depresses me. Why should it depress you, too?"

Lola's eyelids flickered open, and she tugged on her husband, who'd been hovering, causing him to lose his balance and fall onto the couch. Herman squirmed into a seated position and smoothed a hand over his hair before quirking an eyebrow at his bride. "Was that necessary?"

"Nope," Lola answered with a grin. "It was fun, though. Besides, you were taking yourself way too seriously. You had on that long face. All that was missing was someone singing gloom, despair, and agony in the background. Go ahead and tell me what's happening. I'll tell you how to fix it, and we'll both be able to sleep well tonight."

Even though he had misgivings, part of him wanted Lola to make sense of it. Maybe she'd see something he didn't. "Okay, here goes. I think Katie is embezzling."

Lola's expression stayed the same, and then she sniffed and turned to her husband. "Is that it?"

"It's pretty serious." He dropped his chin to keep eye contact with his shorter wife. "We all like Katie and wouldn't like to see anything bad happen to her."

"Wait, wait." Lola held up her hands. "You've all but handcuffed the poor girl. What proof do you have?"

A very good point. Herman raised one finger. "Jake told us she was talking about missing money on the phone in a whisper."

"I was also at the meeting and I heard. It doesn't mean a thing, though. How many embezzlers confide in others about their criminal acts? Seems like a stupid thing to do. It's more likely she's worried she didn't catch this financial chicanery sooner." She balled up her fist and rested her chin on it. "What could be going on with the girl that has her so distracted?"

Herman cleared his throat. "I might know."

"Really?" Lola beamed at her husband. "Do tell, but first get rid of the burnt popcorn. Preferably not in our apartment." She waved her hand in front of her nose. "Open a couple of windows, too."

Anxious to get things sorted out, Herman pushed off the couch and headed into the kitchen to rid the apartment of the offending popcorn. After tossing it in a trash container outside the center, he returned to find the windows already open and Lola sitting on the sofa. She patted the cushion beside her. "Sit down. Tell me what you know."

He perched beside her, intertwining his fingers, and then pushed his clasped hands outward in a stretch. "I bumped into Katie while trying to get another gander at Ron's office."

"Odd. Why was she there?" Lola leaned forward and picked up her laptop from the coffee table. The familiar chortle of the computer powering up sounded.

Herman wrinkled his nose and scratched his head. "Why are you turning on your computer?"

"Multi-tasking. You asked me to check out the former director, so I am. By the way, you're supposed to tell me why Katie's distracted, which you failed to do."

"Getting there. Ron…"

"Ron? He's older than Katie."

"It didn't seem to bother Katie. I caught her in the office gathering up the shoes we thought were his. She explained it was an inside joke. Told me the shoes weren't even his size."

"She knew his shoe size?" Lola narrowed her eyes and firmed her lips. "Anything else?"

Herman recognized his limitations in reading women. Maybe he had misread Katie. "She hugged on the shoes and cried. Tried to act like she wasn't crying. What do you think?"

"Sounds like something might be up between the two of them." She tilted her head to one side as if pondering the situation. "Katie might think they're a love match when Ron didn't. Sometimes, lonely people see things that aren't there. Then there's the possibility that they both tried to keep things quiet. Work romances can get messy."

"Valid reasons," Herman agreed.

Lola pulled out a piece of letterhead from her pocket and smirked at her husband. "You thought I wasn't pulling my weight in this case." She wagged one manicured finger in his face. "I had to get names before I could do anything. So, I can start looking. Besides, I need to find a better person for embezzlement than Katie."

"I hope you do. Boy, do I hope you do." Herman whispered the words, not sure if Lola heard.

Chapter Fifteen

THE MURMUR OF a television news magazine joined the clicking of Lola's manicured nails on the keyboard, creating a discordant chorus. Herman punched his bed pillow and then fluffed it, finally wiggling into a comfortable position on the bed. He cleared his throat and asked, "How much longer are you going to be at this?"

Lola glanced up with her readers sliding down her nose. "You've got no right to complain. First, you're all upset no one is helping you investigate an active case that the local law enforcement can't touch, and then you're upset when I *do* look. It shouldn't take this long to find an accident, especially one as spectacular as the former director's daughter suffered. I heard tell that a semi-truck rolled on her car, crushing every bone in the poor girl's body."

Herman shuddered. "Sounds dreadful. I'm surprised she even survived it."

"Me, too," Lola agreed and then sighed. "Still, I've spent a good hour reviewing the last six months of the local paper. This is the same paper that reports every fire run, police call, marriage, and divorce. Not to mention every name change, which strikes me as counter-productive—and yet, no mention of an accident of that proportion. None."

"Weird." He reached for the remote and changed the channel. A car screamed across the television screen with a squad car in hot pursuit, catching his attention. *This looks promising.*

"Is that all you have to say?" Lola closed her laptop, arched her brows, and pressed her lips together.

Yes, a signal Herman knew well but didn't necessarily know how to translate. He once heard the best way to answer your wife included the line, "You're right, dear."

"What am I right about? I didn't give you an opinion or even a conclusion. I just told you I found no news of an accident and all you say is, 'you're right, dear?'"

The guy who thought "you're right, dear" worked every time deserved a kick in the pants. He'd better be on his toes, then. Herman muted the show. However, he didn't know what to say. Even though television detectives worked wonders with silence, often resulting in the perps confessing all, Herman inherently knew it wouldn't work in this situation. The second technique involved answering a question with a question. "What do you think it means?"

Lola pulled off her readers, exposing narrowed eyes as she rubbed her nose before speaking. "All right, Sherlock, I think there *wasn't* an accident. Apparently, the former director, who happens to be Charmaine Lynch—at least on the letterhead—wanted to make her exit quickly. I'd say the entire story about her daughter and grandchildren is bogus. Her habit of being closemouthed served her well. No one knows if she even had a daughter *or* grandchildren."

"Well, then," Herman suggested, "maybe you need to research Charmaine."

"You're probably right." Lola nodded and covered a yawn with her hand. "Not tonight, though. I've done all I'm going to do.

Tomorrow is another day."

With that announcement, she moved the laptop to the bedside table and turned off the light. Herman turned off the television. Too bad he couldn't turn off his mind—he might as well be a juggler the way he kept throwing possibilities into the air. Now he had to consider Charmaine—not that he'd totally written her off. All the same, if money kept getting shuffled around after her abrupt departure, how could she be guilty? She needed to be guilty because it would clear Katie. Unfortunately, just because you didn't like someone or care overly much about them didn't automatically make them the culprit.

POKER FEVER DESCENDED upon Greener Pastures with the tournament approaching at the end of the week. Residents carried cards in their pockets while others searched online for rules for Texas hold 'em. A few other residents immersed themselves in the poker culture by watching poker-centric movies like *The Cincinnati Kid* and *Casino Royale*.

A fifty-dollar application fee hadn't narrowed down the number of residents wanting to enter. If anything, it increased the number of applicants. No wonder the activity director's normal congenial manner grew frantic and her appearance frazzled as the tournament loomed closer.

Herman strolled past an impromptu poker game taking place in the lobby. At least there'd be no talk about poker at the sleuths' lunch table. All the females would be all a-twitter about the upcoming wedding. He could only hope Gus and Jake would have some information on Ron's whereabouts or at least a clue or two. Even talk about coordinating their ties for the wedding he'd tolerate.

A rich tomato and beef aroma filled the room, making Herman smile. A hearty lunch of spaghetti with meat sauce plus garlic bread brightened any day. The sleuths gathered around the table, engaged in an animated discussion. No one looked up as he approached or even acknowledged him. What could have them so excited? Maybe they knew who set the explosion. As he moved closer, their voices carried.

"Okay, a royal flush is your highest hand, then a straight flush."

"What about bluffing?"

"It's always bluffing since you don't know what cards your opponents are holding."

Good gravy! Not them, too. "Who's entered the tournament?"

Hannah, who'd recently moved into the home, shot her hand up. "I did. I wanted to get involved more with the center and meet more people."

"Likely excuse." Eunice sniffed and raised her chin. "You think you can read up on it and win. Better watch out! I've entered."

Gus spoke out of the side of his mouth. "That's why I *can't* enter. Can't take a chance of playing against Eunice."

It was easy enough to understand why Gus wouldn't take a chance on playing opposite his sweetheart. "I get it," Herman said as he pulled out his chair and sat. "I'm surprised my own dear, sweet bride hasn't entered."

Lola's elegant fingers brushed his hand resting on the table as she purred, "I never said I didn't enter. I felt morally obligated to enter, being from Vegas and all."

Her words froze him for a second, and then Herman smacked his forehead with his hand. "You entered! What about all the times you called the gamblers in Vegas suckers and fools?"

"Oh, they are." She reached for her glass of tea and took a sip before continuing. "In the best of times, you only have a two percent chance of winning. Winning doesn't necessarily mean big money, either. Besides, this will be a friendly competition."

Friendly seldom paired naturally with *competition.*

Chapter Sixteen

A WELCOME SIGHT came in the form of Marcy and Lance strolling through the dining-room door. It even stopped the female sleuths from trash-talking each other in regards to their poker skills. Other residents turned to watch the couple cross the room. A few waved and another called out Marcy's name. Ever gracious, the detective stopped and murmured a few words to folks. The clanking of metal pans and silverware in the kitchen drowned out whatever she said.

"Look at that," Gus grumbled. "It's obvious she came to see us, but everyone has to talk to her. Did they talk to her when she stayed here?"

Perhaps it was meant to be rhetorical, but Herman felt the need to point out the obvious. "Lots of people talked to her while she rehabbed here."

"Yeah. How could I forget?" Gus grimaced. "Some of them constantly circling her like sharks instead of going in for the kill—they just wanted her attention."

A few nods of agreement came from the other sleuths and then a low-voiced comment sounded, possibly of a negative sort. Before Herman could inquire about the nature of it, Marcy and Lance showed at the table. Lance pulled a chair out for Marcy. After she took a seat, Lance located a chair for himself. The two of them grinned at the sleuths, while Marcy put both hands on the table and leaned forward as she spoke. "Guess what?"

"What?" various sleuths asked in unison.

"The Pines wedding chapel had a cancellation."

"Woo-hoo!" Lola chirped, clapping her hands together. "When?"

"This Saturday." Marcy exhaled audibly. "I know it's soon, but they were booked up for the rest of the year. It's just a small wedding and The Pines provides the minister. We show up. You're all invited if you don't have any pressing plans come Saturday."

A chorus composed of *yeses* sounded, all except for Eunice, whose forehead furrowed and her cheeks sucked in as if she'd bitten into an unripe persimmon. "Saturday," she finally said. "This Saturday?"

"That's right," Marcy answered. Her brows arched, but she chose not to inquire. "I realize it's soon. Lance and I already have the license, and we were going to ask a retired judge we both know to help us tie the knot. Then, when the topic of The Pines came up, I thought why not check it out?"

Lance managed a forced laugh. "Someone else's cold feet turned out to be our good luck."

Most of the sleuths chuckled, except for Eunice, who stared straight ahead, possibly gritting her teeth in an effort not to cry. Surely all the sleuths had put together that the wedding and the tournament were on the same day, but not necessarily at the same time. "What time is the wedding?"

"One," Marcy replied, holding her forefinger up. "This place is hopping and technically our ceremony is twenty minutes. We have an extra ten for photos but they have to set up for the next wedding, which is at two. Promptness counts. If you're late, you miss your opportunity to watch." She turned and beamed at Lance as she spoke. "My beloved and I are going to exchange I do's."

In a low voice, possibly not audible to everyone, Eunice grumbled, "The tournament starts at one."

Marcy's smile dimmed a little. "Not everyone has to come. It's not a command performance. Come if you want, but if you've got something else planned, I totally understand. Besides telling you about The Pines, Lance also has news."

If Herman had antennae, they'd vibrate at the possibility of news of the bombing. Perhaps the culprit had demanded a ransom for Ron. "What's up?"

"Since I'm soon to be married," Lance patted his chest to affirm who'd be saying vows, "I need to get cleaned up. A haircut, of course. Marcy even suggested a pedicure. I thought I'd see if any of you would like to go with me."

"I'm not sure…" Gus's hand rubbed his head. "…they can improve on perfection. However, I'm up for a pedicure, especially since I'm not as flexible as I used to be."

Jake and Herman volunteered for haircuts. While spending guy time together, the topic of the explosion might come up. "I might even consider a pedicure," Herman offered.

"Make that a definite," Lola urged with a knowing look. "You need one."

While he knew his wife could be outspoken at times, he didn't expect his toenails to be discussed at the dining room table among friends. "Okay, dear."

"All right." Lance intertwined his fingers. "How long before you're ready to hit the road? I figured I'd drive."

Well aware of the modest sedan Lance normally used, Herman inquired, "Will there be enough room for Marcy?"

Hearing her name, she gestured with her hand as if shooing his concern away. "Don't worry about me. I thought maybe I could learn a little more about wedding rituals. Maybe we could have a little reception here at the center. Not necessarily Saturday, of course. I'm open to a restaurant, too. I thought we could brainstorm like we used to do."

Lola threw up both hands as she said, "Count me in."

"I got you covered with wedding trivia and rituals," Hannah volunteered.

Possibly seeing her chance to be a part of the wedding slipping away, Eunice pointed to herself. "You'll need me to lock in a room for the reception." She held up crossed index and middle fingers. "The activity director and I are like this."

Most everyone knew the activity director made a point of avoiding Eunice due to her grumbling and her grandiose plans for various events. If those crossed fingers symbolized a tree and poison ivy, that made much more sense.

Herman could barely wait to find out what Lance knew. "Okay guys, we should get going. There might be a rush at the barbershop."

"Not before dessert," Gus said, throwing an affronted look Herman's way. "It's oatmeal raisin cookies."

"We can take them with us." Herman realized he'd made a unilateral decision without consulting the owner of the vehicle. "If that's okay with Lance?"

Lance gave a thumbs up.

Their cookies wrapped in napkins, the men stood ready to leave.

As much as Herman wanted to go, he bent low to kiss his wife on the cheek and inquired if she needed anything.

"Go on," Lola said with laughing eyes. "It may be hard to believe, but I can function on my own. Go have fun."

Fun. Not what he had in mind at all.

Chapter Seventeen

A GENTLY GURGLING fountain, along with a small altar with a Buddha statue, greeted the nail patrons on entry. Filmy curtains separated each pedicure chair, except for the two at the end that were saved for couples' or friends' pedicures. It allowed them to converse while enjoying being pampered. The propped-open front door allowed the noxious nail polish odor to escape.

A couple of chairs away, Jake relaxed in a massage chair, wearing a floral shower cap to protect his hair from his mud masque. "At least no one will recognize me like this."

Nearby, Gus, sporting a towel turban, replied, "Why worry? Practically every guy you know is in here." He patted his towel. "Quite frankly, I'm enjoying my shea butter treatment. It will make my noggin as smooth and soft as a baby's butt."

Jake snorted but refused to engage in additional conversation, which allowed Gus to chat with his nail tech, a bubbly Asian girl who looked no more than sixteen. Herman and Lance captured the last two chairs. While their feet soaked, their attendants busied themselves near the front of the salon—a perfect time for Herman to solicit information from Lance.

"Hear anything on Ron?"

Lance tensed up and rolled his shoulders back before answering. "If you're asking me if I found anyone or anything to indicate if Ron showed up the morning of the bombing, then the answer is no."

It was not what he wanted to hear. Herman massaged the back of his neck. "No ransom demands?"

"None," Lance replied, staring straight ahead. "Could be because Ron wasn't taken."

Herman shook his head. "It doesn't make sense. I have to be missing something. Gus never said anything else, which means he doesn't remember. I'm beginning to doubt my own memory."

"It's understandable." Lance leaned awkwardly across the space between the two chairs to pat Herman's arm and then leaned back into his own chair. "This is a normal response. I've had the same reaction when I've tried to recall details about an accident or a getaway car. Things I thought I should remember, I didn't. A couple of times I underwent hypnosis, which helped bring up a few things I'd forgotten."

The possibility hung between the two of them. Every hypnotist Herman ever watched on television made willing participants act the fool. Often, staid older men swished across the stage like beauty queens and other participants crowed like roosters, barked like a dog, or acted like a toddler. "Oh, I don't know. I doubt I could be hypnotized."

"Maybe. Maybe not. You don't know until you try." Lance made eye contact with Herman. "I know you're fond of Ron. I'd think you'd want to do all you could to help him."

"Woo, boy! Talk about a sucker punch." Herman tried for a smile, but the edges wobbled a little. "I guess I should try."

"Good. I know a guy…" Lance teased.

"I bet you do."

Lance pulled out his phone and opened it as he spoke. "With any luck, we might be able to get you hypnotized today."

"Yippee," Herman said in an obviously faked cheery voice. "I can't wait."

★

HERMAN, LANCE, JAKE, and Gus left the salon with trimmed toenails and a relaxed attitude. Gus rubbed his head. "It's like silk." He grabbed Jake's hand and placed it on his head. "Feel it."

Jake jerked away his hand. "I don't want to feel your head."

His appalled attitude made the rest of them laugh all the way to the car. Once ensconced inside the privacy of the car, they joked about the procedures they'd undergone but ultimately admitted they'd relished the experience. Gus surprisingly changed the conversation topic as Lance started the car.

"Did you investigate Claude? I left you several messages about him."

Instead of answering immediately, Lance backed out and then put the car into drive. "Sorry. I wasn't ignoring your calls, but I had nothing to tell you about that. As you've probably guessed, the ATF agents, arson investigator, and the fire marshall handled all that, but I did pass the message along about Claude and heard he was questioned."

"And?" Jake asked since Lance avoided giving any pertinent information.

"Rumor is, since I wasn't in on the questioning, Claude wasn't sophisticated enough to create a bomb that would impact such a small area. I heard he didn't have the wits to make a pipe bomb. Besides, C-4 military-grade explosive was used."

"Aha!" Gus interjected. "That's what I thought it was."

"You did," Herman agreed. Now, if Gus could remember that, maybe he might remember more.

Lance continued his summation. "I'm not sure how Claude could get ahold of that. He alibied out. He was working on a street crew as the flagger. People definitely would have missed him."

"What about…" Gus leaned forward from the back seat to speak almost in Lance's ear. "…his threat to burn the center to the ground when he was fired?"

"Burn, not bomb," Lance pointed out. "He's a mouthy little slacker. No gumption or smarts to be much of a threat."

"That's no help," Gus complained and plopped back into his seat. "That leaves us with nothing."

"Not exactly nothing," Lance added. "A little blood showed up in our search of Ron's office. Currently, they're running tests—I assume. All my information is second-hand."

Herman, who managed to snag the shotgun seat, wondered aloud, "Do you think the explosion could possibly be entwined with the embezzling?"

The car jerked, causing their seatbelts to lock as Lance stepped on the brake and demanded, "What embezzling?"

"No embezzling!" Jake yelled, giving Herman a slap on the shoulder and a preventative poke for Gus. "The guys just misheard something. You know them. Everything is a crime drama. This is all based on a random remark about there being a pet therapy account and no pet therapy. It could be it hasn't started yet. These things take time."

The most normal thing would be to pump them for information, but Lance continued to drive while murmuring, "No problem.

Embezzlement isn't my wheelhouse anyhow. Usually, the FBI investigates that kind of thing. Besides, I have an upcoming wedding."

Chapter Eighteen

CAR HORNS BLASTING indicated an increase in traffic and unhappy or possibly impatient motorists. Lance wove through the traffic with a confident air, while Herman fiddled with his shirt cuffs, contemplating the upcoming hypnosis session. "I didn't even see you call the hypnotist."

"No need," Lance replied, keeping his eyes on the road. "I already contacted Michael on the off-chance you might agree. Sent a text at the salon."

"Pretty confident I'd say yes."

"Not at all. But it pays to be prepared. In the end, if you do remember something significant, we hand it over to the other guys and hope they do things right."

"It stinks," Jake offered from the back seat, adding a grunt to underscore his opinion.

Gus leaned forward and pointed to the embedded lights in the dashboard. "How about turning on the lights and siren to cut through the traffic?"

"No need." Lance spoke in his usual calm voice. He glanced into the rearview mirror, spotting the expected mischievous expression. "What might be fun for you could end up in major censure for me. Already, I'm courting a scolding by marrying my partner because the implication would be we were romantically involved, which is against regulation. If a person wants to date a co-worker, someone needs to transfer out. Can't have a cop or detective so worried about the welfare of their partner that the criminal escapes."

"I can see that," Gus said but made an odd face in the mirror by stretching his mouth wide as if screaming before continuing. "Once you're married, it's obvious you're involved, or were."

"You're not wrong. They figure by that time, the romance has dimmed a little, allowing a person to concentrate on their job. Married partners seldom work together. The only exception might be a town so small they only have a few peace officers."

Even though the discussion about romance in the workforce kept Herman mildly distracted, he kept chewing on what might happen. Ideally, he'd remember an important detail his memory inconveniently tucked away. Worst case scenario would be he'd remember nothing, wasting everyone's time. His hands fisted as he stared out the window at the multitude of fast-food restaurants, gas stations, and tire stores popping up like dandelions. "Things have certainly got built up around here."

"Yep," Gus agreed. "Decades ago, this was nothing but a cow path meandering between fenced-in fields. Farmers would own an acre here and there. They'd herd the cows to the next pasture after they'd finished off the current one."

Herman let out a slow breath, relating to the cows being herd-ed—the only difference between the two of them was he could almost swear his current direction wouldn't serve him or the case. Before he could mention this, the click of the turn signal indicated an immediate change as the car slowed and veered to the left onto a residential street. Trees lined the initial road entrance. A steep hill caused a mechanical groan as Lance goosed the gas pedal. The vehicle showed reluctance, possibly channeling Herman's feelings.

On top of the hill, a half-dozen houses lined both sides of the road, varying from a rustic log cabin to neat brick ranches with towering pine trees marking the lot boundaries. Lance continued on until he reached a long drive, flicked on his signal, slowed, and turned into the curving driveway. Gold, rust, and burgundy mums overflowed from stone pots fronting an expansive veranda. Lace curtains shielded long windows on an older home reminiscent of those of Herman's childhood. It was not the house he expected from a grizzled law enforcement veteran. Apparently, his wife had fancied up the place.

The car stopped, but before they could all pile out, Lance twisted in his seat to address those in the back. "This is a serious matter. No teasing or goofing around."

Gus jerked his head back as if slapped. He pointed to himself with a backward thumb. "Me? Don't be silly. You must mean Jake."

Jake shoved him, causing Lance to sigh heavily. "This is exactly what I mean. If you can't be quiet during the hypnosis, you're welcome to stay in the car."

This shut both men up. Unfortunately, it only tensed Herman up, knowing what his two buddies were capable of doing.

Gus held up three fingers with his pinkie and thumb folded at the base of his hand. "I'll behave. Scout's honor."

If the scouts had allowed a young Gus within their ranks, he may not have stayed long. Herman chose to say nothing, concentrating on breathing through his nose in deep, long breaths—the type of breathing the guy on the meditation video assured would bring on relaxation and passage to a higher realm. So far, nothing. When they swung the car doors open, they could hear songbirds singing, which could be a positive sign. By the time Herman reached the steps leading up to the veranda, two jays in a nearby tree engaged in a fight.

The door opened before Lance even knocked. A fifty-ish woman with an ash blonde bob and attired in a floral dress nodded in Lance's direction. "Looks to me like you brought me multiple clients. I may have to charge you the bulk rate."

Lance chuckled. "Just one, Michael. The other two will observe, silently."

"Michael?" Jake repeated the name as if unsure that he'd heard right. "Not Michelle?"

The woman stepped back to allow them entrance into the foyer lined with photos of three children in various stages of life. "Oh, it's just Michael. I was one of those surprise babies after my parents accepted there'd be no one to carry on the family name. Once they decided to name me after my father, it never occurred to them I might be a girl. I guess you might say they weren't able to deal with sudden change, which explains why my name is Michael. It's not so bad, especially when I get to see expressions like yours. Follow me. I'll take you to the treatment room."

They weaved past overstuffed furniture, fresh flowers in vases, and a fireplace mantle decorated with wooden deer in varied poses. She opened a door, revealing a room with a draped window, no wall art, and two straight back chairs in the middle. A small table with a lamp stood next to the chairs.

It could be an interrogation room. Why did Herman think he'd be sitting in a soft chair with a fountain nearby? There were a couple of other chairs against the wall, which meant others came to wait or watch.

Michael glanced at the extra chairs. "Oh, there aren't enough. I can get an extra one from the kitchen."

"No problem," Lance told her. "I can stand. I don't think it will take too long."

"All right." Michael gestured to the chairs against the wall. Gus grabbed one and moved it close to the middle.

"If it's okay, I want to observe, but I've been warned not to speak."

Michael glanced back at Lance and then nodded at Gus. "Sounds okay to me. Hypnosis is a simple process of prodding your unconscious mind to release details. There's nothing secretive or magical about it. I'll explain as I go along. Since you know my name, it would be helpful if I know yours."

Each sleuth introduced himself with Herman going last. He pointed to the chair facing Michael. "I guess I'm supposed to sit there?"

"Yes, if you would. It's a pleasure meeting all of you. I'm going to close the door and turn on a white noise machine outside the door. This is to drown out any noise my cats might make. It's hard to remember something when you hear odd noises nearby. It's also the reason I chose a room the farthest away from road sounds."

Herman sat and forced himself to breathe evenly—if not to calm himself, to convince the guys he could handle this. Michael turned on the small lamp before pulling the door closed. Despite being daytime, the room became shadowy with only the lamp serving as an illuminated beacon. Even Michael remained half in shadows with the side nearest the light being visible. It reminded Herman of one of those comic book villains like Two-Face. How could he concentrate with part of her face veiled?

Michael started. "The reason I use a plain room, plain chairs, and just a spot of light is to help focus. Too many distractions send our minds racing. Ironically, teachers often paper rooms with bright colors and motivational posters, hoping to provide a creative environment. For too many students, it's a chaotic environment. For those who've suffered trauma, which you all have, the calmer, less distractive the environment, the better." She pulled out her phone, selected an app, and held it up. "I usually record the experience. Most people want to listen because it's easy to forget what is said. Do I have your permission?"

Herman bobbed his head, finding his mouth dry.

She set the phone on the nearby table as she started. "Let's go back to the day of the bombing. What kind of a day was it?"

Herman bit his lip. Was this it? What about the shiny object that would pull him into a deeper state as it swung back and forth? The words burst from his mouth. "No pocket watch?"

"I do have something similar." Michael reached for a small box on the lamp table and extracted a cone-shaped object hanging from a slender chain. Light reflected off the copper-colored cone and chain as it swung slowly. "Are you comfortable?"

Herman wiggled in his chair. "About as good as I can be."

"Take three deep breaths."

Herman took a deep breath and then let it go slowly. He repeated the procedure twice more and then concentrated on the object swinging slowly in front of him.

In a soft voice, Michael said, "It's natural to have different thoughts crowded into your mind. Think of them as balloons. Nothing is wrong with them, but they're not needed here. Let them go, watch them drift away."

Behind him, Herman could hear heavy breathing. He wondered if Gus had fallen asleep. If so, he'd better not snore and totally ruin the mood. Michael spoke again. "Go back a few days. What do you remember?"

While Herman scoured his mind for something he may have missed, Gus's voice spoke in a slow, low voice, totally different from his usual patter.

"A normal day, no different than most. I didn't expect to discover what I did."

Lance abandoned his casual lounging position against the wall and moved closer once Gus spoke. Leave it to Gus to upstage Herman, but maybe his buddy accidentally became hypnotized and could now remember what happened.

Michael glanced back at Lance, who nodded at her to continue, which she did. "What did you discover?"

"Someone I trusted, a person with whom I shared my innermost secrets, was a murderer."

Eunice? That's the only person Herman could think of. While she could be opinionated, acerbic, and cheated at bingo, she wasn't a murderer. What could he mean? Shadows hid Jake's expression. It would be hard to measure if Jake knew anything. Lance practically vibrated, trying to remain still and yet take in information.

Michael, her voice soft and melodic, inquired, "Who? Who's the murderer?"

"Maybe I am due to not being suspicious earlier. If I had, maybe this could have been prevented. It just never occurred to me that Cleo would react in such a manner."

"Cleo?" Jake's shocked, loud voice came from the dark, startling everyone, including Gus, who slipped from his chair.

Herman turned immediately and reached out a helping hand to

LATE FOR THE WEDDING

his friend. "You, okay?"

Instead of answering, Gus sat on the floor, blinking. "Why am I on the floor?"

"You fell out of your chair right after you told us Cleo is the murderer. Who's Cleo?"

Gus grabbed Herman's hand and accepted assistance. Once resettled in his chair, he rubbed a hand over his face. "What happened? Were you hypnotized?"

"Sadly, no," Herman admitted. "But you were. We all want to know about Cleo."

Gus sucked in his lips and shook his head. "I don't know anyone by that name."

Perhaps feeling Herman was failing at pulling information from Gus, Lance moved closer and dropped to his haunches, putting himself at eye level. "You said, 'Someone I trusted, a person whom I shared my innermost secrets with, was a murderer.'"

"Hmmm," Gus murmured, tilting his head a little. "Sounds familiar. Did I say anything else?"

"You were guilty because you weren't initially suspicious."

Gus's brow furrowed as he wrung his hands—not normal behavior for the jovial man. The white of his eyes flashed as he engaged in playing tag with an elusive memory. "What you said sounds so familiar, but it eludes me."

Michael, who stayed silent during the exchange, inquired, "Would you like me to try hypnosis again?"

Both Lance and Herman agreed, but despite a willingness to try, nothing came of it. Instead, they left the house all wondering about Cleo. Could she be an actual person Gus knew or maybe a dream that felt real? If nothing else, they should check if anyone named Cleo either worked at the center or lived there.

Chapter Nineteen

UNCERTAINTY DRAPED OVER the car's occupants, similar to a thick fog obscuring everything. The playful attitude that prevailed during the nail salon treatment faded with Gus's cryptic remark about Cleo and Herman's failure to be hypnotized and contribute anything of value. When people depended on him, he tended to let them down. Herman inhaled deeply, trying to calm himself. He turned slightly to judge if his buddies suffered from similar stress as he did, only to find them both slumped against each other, fast asleep with their mouths slightly ajar.

That just left Lance and himself as the only two awake in the car. He should say something as opposed to brooding. "So, where have the agents set up camp?"

"At our station," Lance replied, wrinkling his nose. "Marcy gave up her office for them. Claimed she wasn't solving many crimes by answering the phone. Someone might as well use it."

"Very thoughtful," Herman commented with a nod. On most of the crime dramas, the local police were not so accommodating. They usually stood on the sidelines and griped about the outsiders loud enough for the non-locals to hear. "Not sure I'd give up my office."

Lance chuckled, clearing his throat. "She gave up her office, in theory. In truth, she keeps returning to it to get items."

"And eavesdrop," Herman added with a grin.

"You got that right." He barked laughter and then inhaled before shaking his head. "Technically, we locals are supposed to be kept in the informational loop. More than likely, when any of those alphabet soup folks come in, they keep their hunches and theories close to their chests. They want to be a hundred percent certain before announcing their results. It helps prevent egg on their faces."

Normally, Herman tended to be the sleuth who crossed his t's and dotted his i's. Without his serving as an anchor, Gus and Eunice's wild suppositions and boundless confidence would end up with them in jail. On the other hand, the unchecked duo did unearth clues. A twinge of envy stabbed at him like an annoying gremlin. What if Gus nailed the case with the mention of Cleo? How could he know any of this? Herman saw all the same stuff as Gus. To shake off his mood, Herman wiggled his shoulders while trying to think of something pertinent to contribute to the conversation. "Is anything ever a hundred percent?"

Lance shot him an approving look. "Exactly. Some of the blanks can't be filled in because they don't know the town and how it works. Those could easily be answered by a local LEO."

Snores drifted from the back seat. Herman narrowed his eyes and considered his sleeping buddies behind him. A tiny window of opportunity opened up, allowing him to know something the other two didn't. Sure, he might only have the information for a couple of hours at the most. He inhaled deeply and fisted his hands, certain that Jake would wake up in time to comment. In a low voice, he asked, "Did Marcy hear anything interesting?"

Even though Lance made a point of keeping his eyes on the road, his voice swung up higher than his normal baritone. "You betcha. Blood."

"Blood." Herman echoed the word. "I went into the room and shot photos. I didn't see anything."

"There wasn't much to see, actually. A spot about the size of a dime. We tested it."

"And?" Herman prompted. "You're not going to leave *me* hanging, are you?"

"You know better than that." Lance checked his mirrors and turned on his signal as he switched lanes.

Familiar with the area, Herman knew there wasn't much time before they reached the center, and they'd all spill out of the car like puppies—make that arthritic puppies, smelling of the salon's cedarwood and rosemary lotion. "I do."

"Well," Lance started and then stopped as a rusted-out sedan with a missing muffler shot past him going at least twenty miles over the speed limit. His lips twisted and he reached for his radio and called it in. "The fool will probably be in a ditch if he's lucky before the patrol car catches up with him."

New Albany numbered as many bad drivers as most cities of equal size. Be that as it may, Herman wanted to know about the blood and preferably before his buds woke up. It would be great to have a juicy tidbit like that to share.

A call came in on the radio asking for more information. Lance responded to it while Herman alternated between staring at his friends to ascertain their state of slumber and shifting impatiently in his seat. As for the backseat buddies, it wouldn't be the first time they pretended to be asleep. Often acting confused allowed them to wiggle out of troublesome situations that would land younger whippersnappers in big trouble. Another tool in the old person's tool chest was to feign sleep to get out of things. People normally tiptoed away.

Herman waited a few seconds after Lance ended the call. "Did they get a match on the blood?"

"Yes." Lance frowned and scratched his neck. "Stacey Reuben."

The name failed to ring any bells. It might as well be Cleo. Here he thought he knew everyone at the center. "Does Stacey Reuben have a record?"

"Nope, just the opposite. Apparently, he was a much-decorated career service fellow. Army, since I knew you'd ask. We have a DNA profile because he did one of those ancestry hunts. I have to say, everyone searching to see if their great-great-grandpa was either an aristocrat or a horse thief has been a boon to law enforcement. Serial killers have even been tracked down due to wanting to trace their family tree."

"I don't recognize the name," Herman admitted with a bit of a grumble in his voice. Nothing seemed to help. Whatever clues they came up with just brought up more questions. "Can't they go talk to Stacey?"

"There's the problem." Lance pressed his lips together, squinting a little. "Stacey Reuben died about five years ago. Military funeral and all."

As complications went, the death of the suspect headed the list. There was a good chance zombies weren't visiting Greener Pastures. Not knowing what to say, Herman said nothing.

Chapter Twenty

T HE LATE AFTERNOON sun dipped behind the center buildings, throwing out long shadows. A silence hung between Lance and Herman as the sedan turned into the parking lot. There was not much a person could say without bringing up the undead or zombies and risk sounding foolish when it came to Stacey Reuben, a man who merited a full military funeral. Appearing silly never bothered Gus, who interjected, "What if it's someone with the same name?"

Jake, who must have been jostled awake by his companion, managed a derisive snort. "No way they could have the same DNA."

On that point, Herman would concur. Forensic use of DNA started in the late 1980s and didn't happen without a few fumbles. Instead of being the end all that crime dramas portrayed it to be, it more or less helped to eliminate folks as opposed to fingering the guilty party. Usually, only criminals had DNA collected.

Most folks who committed a single crime and left DNA behind would still be hard to trace. Jobs often required fingerprinting, but few asked for DNA. The guilty party might go on to lead an exemplary life, not attracting a second glance. Often, when people were arrested for past crimes, their neighbors often served as their most vocal defenders. Instead of entering the conversation, he allowed Lance, the only professional in the car, to handle it.

"You're right," Lance agreed as he guided the car into a nearby parking space. "He could be in the same family as Stacey Reuben and have the same genetic markers. The only sample submitted to the DNA registry was Stacey's. I can't say if it was an exact match because Marcy couldn't hang around for the conversation without looking obvious."

"I hear you," Jake commented, while Herman played with various scenarios before asking, "How old can a DNA sample be and still offer test results?"

In his mind, he imagined Stacey Reuben dropping by to see a relative. Perhaps he asked to see the director, upset his kin didn't receive a requested soda at night or some other triviality. While in the office, he suffered a paper cut or a nose bleed, leaving DNA behind. A fistfight over a forgotten soda felt like too much. Maybe they should be looking for relatives of Reuben living at Greener Pastures.

Lance unbuckled his seat belt and bit his lip before addressing the question. "It all depends on the decay rate. Sunlight, heat, oxygen, and water speed up the decay. Most samples out in the elements fade away in about a month, but mummies or bones preserved in a cool, dry, dark place last much longer. Even before we had DNA testing, officers were preserving samples for when we would be able to test it."

It was not exactly what he wanted to hear. "I guess expecting a drop of blood saved five years ago to be testable isn't realistic."

Always courteous, Lance managed a sympathetic smile. "There's a lot I don't know about the sample, but it was located on a blotter style desk calendar, which happened to be on the current month."

A heavy sigh escaped Herman. All their cold cases had depended on using the old gray matter. They'd read the notes the detectives had penned and stared at the crime photos. For a few cases, they were able to visit the scene, albeit long after the crime. Unfortunately, there were no notes now, and apparently, no one was sharing information. Solving this would depend on asking questions. He didn't know the right ones to ask. "That ruins my theory."

"Besides," Jake offered from the back. "The housekeeping staff would be fairly inept if they missed cleaning up blood."

"Remember," Gus prompted, wagging his index finger up. "The blood happened to be on a paper calendar, which the staff *couldn't* clean up. Besides, they probably didn't mess with the desk. Folks tend to get irate when you move things around on their desk. I can testify to that."

Even though that sounded like a teaser for a story, Herman refused to bite. What he really needed was to return to his room and boot up his laptop. Surely there had to be some information on Stacey Reuben and his family.

Lance, who hadn't heard Gus's complete collection of far-fetched stories making him sound like a cross between Huckleberry Finn and Dennis the Menace, encouraged the telling. "I'd love to hear it."

Aware the tales could grow a little long-winded, Herman patted his pockets. "Oops, it's a notification. It's Lola."

Jake, possibly up to Herman's machinations, teased, "I didn't hear anything."

"I had it on vibrate during the hypnosis session." He pulled out his phone and cupped his left hand around it to prevent anyone from spying on his non-message. "Oh, it *is* from Lola." He made sure to furrow his brow as he continued, "She needs my help. I need to go right away."

Jake leaned forward and asked, "Did she say anything about Hannah?"

He could say nothing, but that would be rude. If nothing else, the Army taught him to help out a fellow soldier. "Hmmm," he pretended to read a text. "I'm not sure. That H word *might* be Hannah. Let me put on my readers to be sure."

"Don't bother," Jake said as he swung open the car door. "I appreciate the ride and the walk on the spa side. The girls have no clue what we guys have to do to stay handsome." He exited the car with more energy than he'd shown in a month.

"Ah…" Herman stalled, not sure how to make a gracious exit.

"Go on," Gus said. "Go do your pretend errand. I'm certain Eunice will survive without my company for the next ten, fifteen minutes, or however long it takes to relate my tale."

Even though he felt bad for Lance, he touched his shoulder as he unbuckled his safety belt. "I appreciate everything you did for me today. Everything. I'm only sorry it didn't work out better."

Chapter Twenty-One

AFTER BEING INSIDE the car with its tinted windows and dim interior, Herman stumbled to a halt inside Greener Pasture's lobby doors. The excess of overhead illuminations and the PA system blaring a call for a custodian assaulted his senses. In a few seconds, his pupils would constrict and the obnoxious message would finish. Some folks put their mouth too close to the phone and then raised their voice as if they had to be heard across the center without any audio magnification. Two female residents chattered to the left of him. One mentioned waiting for a pizza.

Elsewhere, a receptionist might have accepted a delivery and then called the resident. This thought had him glancing to his right, expecting to see the top of the receptionist's head as she played with her phone. Not today, though, because the receptionist conversed with a well-dressed gentleman somewhere on the good side of fifty. With his back to Herman, he couldn't determine much more.

The same receptionist, who couldn't even comment on the bombing or seeing Ron, paid plenty of interest to the man, which probably made him good-looking or important. An envelope appeared on the receptionist's desk—she immediately placed her hand over it and slid it off. Curious.

Herman may have stared at her a bit too long, noticing her full eyebrows and thick eyeliner. It reminded him a bit of the Cleopatra film done years ago. She must have noticed his interest because she barked, "Do you need help?"

Yes, definitely too long. "Ah, no…" Herman blinked a couple of times. "Takes time for my eyes to grow accustomed to the change in light when I come in from the outside."

The man turned at the comment, giving Herman the once-over. Anxious to leave, Herman gave a nod in acknowledgment and headed for his apartment. As he walked away, he fought the desire to turn and look some more. However, he didn't want the man to notice him. The stranger wasn't handsome. A sense of menace wafted from him. Any thinking person would keep far away from him. Blame it on his dead eyes that showed no spark of kindness. He seemed more machine than human. Why did the receptionist appear so animated with him nearby? It could be the envelope and its contents. The place he thought he knew so well became one mystery after another.

His apartment beckoned him rather like a mirage of an oasis in a desert. Unlike the mirage, he'd reach his apartment, boot up his computer, and find some answers.

"Herman, wait!"

Manners had him stopping and turning, spotting his quick-to-leave pal. Jake caught up with him by taking a few lunging steps.

"Hey." Herman greeted him, a little reluctantly. "Thought you were going to help Hannah."

"Yeah…" Jake's hand went up to rub his neck. "…me, too. The woman is nowhere to be found, and she tends to be unpredictable." He shrugged his shoulders. "More time for you and I to brainstorm. We should stop by Katie's office and tell her the names we need her to look up."

While they were there, they might as well mention what they were doing, too. It shouldn't raise her suspicions if she had nothing to hide. Guilty people should always be on guard, never knowing when someone might recognize their smokescreen. One wrong step or a wrong word to the wrong person could cause their fake persona to tumble down like a mortarless brick wall. Personally, he'd rather not involve Katie. If she'd gotten herself into trouble, maybe she could get herself out of it. "Let's not bother her. I'm sure she has plenty to do without running errands for us."

He exhaled audibly, not hiding his frustration with Herman's response. "It would be easier to have Katie look it up. She wouldn't tell *me* no." He sucked in his lips and shook his head. "Wouldn't be fair of me, though. She's rattled enough, afraid something isn't quite right with the books. When they hired her, she commented once she thought it was odd since they already had Arnold as an accountant and places of this size seldom need more than one. She complained Arnold would let her do very little with the major accounts, making her more of a Girl Friday and letting her handle only a few lesser accounts. Then he died," Jake slapped his hands together, "just like that. Heard he was only forty-nine. I would have assumed older due to his receding hairline. Anyhow, he left things in a bit of a mess. Katie didn't have his laptop or anything. If she had, one of those geek fellows could have hacked into it. Mainly, she's been playing catch up, trying to match the money coming in to the money going out."

Arnold of the receding hairline. Herman tried to place him. "Anything else unusual about him? I'm trying to remember him."

"He wore glasses. Not a good look with his hairline, either. A bit of a paunch that those dark suits he preferred to wear did nothing to hide." Jake twisted his lips to one side, showing his feelings about the man's lack of fashion sense.

The dark suit remark made him remember the man in the lobby similarly attired, but his suit probably cost much more. "Did you notice the man in the lobby talking to the receptionist when you entered?"

"Stopped me in my tracks." His eyebrows arched as he spoke. "Who wears a Dior suit in this burg?"

It sounded like a rhetorical question to him and he had no clue who Dior was. All the same, maybe he should answer. "Who?"

"Never mind. Until today, I've only seen those suits on celebrities on television. Depending on the suit, they easily run three thousand bucks or more."

An oxford shirt and khakis suited most occasions. The suit Herman used for his and Lola's wedding he had bought at the mall and counted himself lucky to find it on sale and washable. "Whoa! That's a lot of money. Can't believe someone would spend so much. Why?"

Jake made a tsking noise and then inserted both hands into his pockets and smirked. "Most men who pay that kind of money because they can and to impress people."

"It only works if people know enough about clothes to know it's expensive. It doesn't change the person he is. Clothes can only do so much. *I'm* not impressed."

"I can see that." Jake nudged Herman as he moved closer. "I think this is a conversation best not conducted in a public hallway."

The two of them nodded at a passing staff member as they

strolled down the corridor. The hiss of the wall deodorizer unit caused Herman to startle, bumping into his buddy.

"You're wound pretty tight. A person might think *you* were the one getting married." Jake laughed at his own joke. "Funny, right?"

"Not really," Herman said, fanning away the cloud of scent. "I have nothing against the idea of scent, but this one smells like bleach and laundry soap."

"That might be cotton or linen. Something like cedar or pine would be refreshing and woodsy."

"Yep." Herman offered the agreement knowing Jake preferred that as opposed to a debate on various air fresheners. He probably preferred people to agree with everything he said while Gus enjoyed a good debate. Not that Gus would ever consider himself a loser when it came to a debate. He'd proudly announce he'd agree to disagree.

Jake and Herman's shared stroll carried them to the apartment where Lola opened the door. "Hello, boys." She dusted a kiss on her husband's cheek before brandishing a blue rhinestone barrette. "I'm off. We're trying to round up something old, something new, something borrowed, something blue, and a penny for her shoe for Marcy. I found something blue. Better get back there before anyone returns with something blue. I don't want to get stuck with the penny."

Both men moved aside to allow Lola to pass. After she did, Herman entered and waited for Jake to do so before closing and locking the door. "I'd better get some paper and a pen. I was just going to look up Reuben's name, but everything is stacking up fast."

"Like what?" Jake asked as he strolled to the fridge, opened it, and peered inside. "How come you don't have any ginger ale?"

"I don't like it. *You* like it." His computer rested on the table. A tablet with a couple of pens completed his research supplies. Once seated, he called back to Jake, "Bring me a cream soda!"

The familiar chime sounded as the computer booted up along with Jake grumbling as he brought the drinks. "I don't know a grown man who drinks cream soda."

"Sure, you do. Me." Herman refused to buy into Jake's concern about manly choices. After all, Herman won Lola's heart without expensive suits or masculine drink choices. He flipped open the tablet with a thump. "What was Arnold's last name?"

"Don't know," Jake said and then took a long drink of his root beer. "Katie only called him Arnold around me."

"The last name might be good to know, especially if someone embezzled. Arnold should have known about the embezzling."

"Could have been Arnold." Jake raised his soda can as if saluting the possibility.

"He's dead. The embezzling could still be happening." A light bulb popped on in the old figuring-out-stuff department. He picked up the pen and wrote *Arnold*, and then *death* with a dash. "How did he die?"

"Aneurysm. One day he was fine, the next day, dead."

"Convenient," Herman muttered to himself as he wrote.

"How can an aneurysm be convenient?" Jake squinted over his soda can.

Wanting Katie not to be involved in the embezzlement, he'd grab at anything, no matter how ludicrous. "What if Arnold was embezzling and someone found out? They arranged a little…" He put up his fingers to make air quotes. "…accident."

"Really…" Jake pushed out the word through pursed lips as though he'd prefer another word. "Have you been watching those mob movies, thinking everyone who dies has been rubbed out?"

When put that way, it did seem silly. "What if he *was* the embezzler? His death wouldn't serve anyone. Couldn't even collect all the money he tucked away. If he did hide some money, where is it?"

Herman picked up his pen again and wrote feverishly as he continued to speak. "Was he married? He could have left instructions for his family in case of death. For all we know, they could have headed out to the Caribbean by now."

"You may have something there." Jake placed his soda on the table, placed his elbows on the table, and rested his chin in an upturned palm. His gaze fixed on the closed door for several seconds before he jerked upright. "I've got it!"

"What?" Herman straightened, too, feeling a kick of energy surging through him. This must be how a bloodhound felt when picking up a scent. Before long, he'd be tracking down a bomber, an embezzler, or maybe a murderer who could make murder resemble a natural cause.

"The website!" Jake exclaimed with a gleam in his eyes, hinting at a great discovery. "Hannah complained many of the things advertised on the website no longer exist at the center because no one has bothered to update it. On the other hand, things we do have aren't listed, either."

The surge of energy died a quick death. Now he knew the disappointment of only finding an empty candy wrapper as opposed to the trail of the culprit. He blew out a long breath, not exactly calming, but he did it more to express his current mindset, sounding a bit like a raspberry.

"It's not the very first time a website advertisement inaccurately portrayed a property or activity." Why Jake thought this important puzzled him. They all had strong points and Jake could detect patterns in random things, possibly due to flying and peering at the faraway landscape and trying to decipher his location. "Okay, I give. What about the website has you so worked up?"

A smile pulled his friend's skin almost tight and he held up one hand as if testifying. "Arnold's name should be on the website along with a few others. They even had a directory under contacts." He managed a sage nod and added, "We might even find Cleo."

Suddenly, Herman found himself grinning like the Cheshire cat in *Alice in Wonderland*. He'd definitely caught the scent again.

Chapter Twenty-Two

ACTIVITIES AND THE residents at Greener Pastures slowed down as the day lengthened. Most of the inhabitants retired to their rooms to await dinner. A few pop-up games of bridge occurred in various lounges. A resident-led book club debated the merits of *The Alice Network* on C Wing. In one apartment, two senior sleuths attempted to solve a crime with almost no significant clues.

Herman carefully printed names from the center's old website onto his paper, his pen squeaking as he did so. Silence surrounded him, except for Jake fiddling with the salt and pepper shakers. He slid the napkin holder one way and then used his thumb to move the sugar bowl closer to an empty soda can. Part of him half-wondered what his friend's antics signified. Rather than ask, Herman compartmentalized the actions, reminding himself to ask later. Right now, he needed to concentrate on the names and what they represented.

"Arnold Truman," he murmured the name. "Talk about a name that doesn't fit."

Jake paused in arranging the table accessories. "What do you mean? Plenty of people are named Truman. We even had a president named that. What are you mumbling about?"

"All names we have currently have changed over the years. Some are about physical characteristics such as small, long, or big. Others tell of locations—where someone lived. Others reflect on the nature of the man such as Truman, which could be separated into *true* and *man*, which would imply an honest person. Didn't you say Katie complained the fellow was secretive?"

Jake sat up a little straighter and then glanced up at the ceiling. "Well, truthfully, she didn't say that to me. I heard her complaining to one of her girlfriends on the phone. She said Arnold was paranoid. Always hovered over his work like a first grader guarding a test paper. He made a point of turning his desk opposite of hers to keep Katie from seeing anything. Sounds odd, but not dishonest."

"Maybe," Herman agreed, but he tugged on his ear, not entirely convinced. Sure, Arnold could be resentful that a new person had suddenly shown up in his office. The real question would be why hire Katie if they didn't need help? Before he could inquire, a lively tap sounded on the exterior door. He opened his hand and dropped his face into it. *Gus.*

"I know you're in there! Lola told me."

Of course, she did. The handle rattled a little, demonstrating Gus's determination to get inside. "Now, that's just dirty, locking me out."

Jake cut his eyes to Herman since, as the official resident, he should make the call. He pushed out from the table, unlocked the door, and opened it. "For your information, I wasn't locking you out, but those who feel free to peer in to see if the old folks are still kicking."

"I hear you," Gus said, strolling into the room with a jaunty step. His steps carried him past the table to the fridge which he opened and inspected, pulling out a jar of pickles. "You're sorely lacking in snacks. You need to get that big land yacht you call a car out and go to the grocery."

"You could bring your own snacks, too," Herman prompted, used to his friends free-loading as he retook his seat.

"I could," Gus cheerfully agreed and pulled a pickle spear from the jar and crunched into it. While chewing loudly, he waved the uneaten pickle portion in Jake's direction. "Did I tell you about my latest podcast?" Before anyone could reply, Gus continued, alternating talking about his current podcast and finishing off the dill spear. "They take a crime and then dramatize it like a play, taking various parts. It's usually people talking about the killer they knew. There's this one about…"

Gus paused and withdrew his phone, scrolled, squinted, and then held out his left hand to Herman, who handed over his readers. "Ah, here it is—*The Deadly Dorm Mother*. Everyone thinks Cleo is the perfect person to…" he stopped when he caught Jake and Herman exchanging pointed glances. "What's with the weird expressions?"

"Cleo," Jake and Herman managed to say in unison.

"Yeah, what about it?" Gus cocked his head like a bird listening for a worm and then handed the readers back.

People sometimes didn't remember things when they were hypnotized, which explained the use of a tape recorder. Herman cleared his throat. "When we were at the hypnotist, you mentioned Cleo and not having a clue she was guilty, or something like that."

"Yeah," Jake added and then grumbled, "You had us chasing our tails trying to find someone named Cleo."

"It explains why we didn't." Herman tapped the tablet that included the names of people of interest. "Just as well. What if we did find a Cleo and turned the information over to Lance, who'd hand it to the ATF guys? The poor woman's life would be ruined trying to prove her innocence."

"Ah, about that." Gus put down the pickle jar and stumbled back a few feet, placing his opened hands at waist level as if to stop the accusations. "Hey, the podcast was in *my* memory. They make a decent show of it. It really does feel like you're there, especially when I use those cordless earbuds. Could one of you call Lance and explain it was just a podcast?"

Herman shook his head no while Jake offered a possibility. "I'm not certain Lance believed the Cleo thing. Besides, as a man on the verge of a life-altering transition, he'd overlook your fumble."

Gus exhaled audibly and grimaced. "Lance would never reprimand me. You can bet when they play good cop, bad cop with a suspect, he's always the nice one." He shuffled his feet, inserted his hands into his pockets, and rattled his change. "It's not that. Don't want to be that old guy who doesn't have it altogether. Can't tell reality from a podcast."

"At least you were hypnotized," Herman pointed out. "As for me, I got nothing. Before you go getting all down on yourself, everyone makes mistakes. What if a young guy did likewise?"

Gus pulled out a kitchen chair and plopped down into it. He leaned back a little and relaxed his shoulders. "That's right, even the young make mistakes. No doubt they make quite a few of them."

"Yep," Jake said with a sparkle in his eye. "They usually call it a senior moment, too." He reached over to poke Gus with his finger. "Got you."

While the two enjoyed playing jokes on each other, it could get a little thin at times. Herman needed to get them back on track. "We have names to investigate."

The unit door crashed open, drawing their attention to a red-faced Lola. She wielded her cane more like a cudgel as she planted it hard on the carpet, slamming the door. Herman, who'd never witnessed his wife this upset, scoured his limited mental resources on how to handle an angry female. Unfortunately, he had nothing.

Gus, not invested in the relationship, called out. "Woo, wee! You came in here like an out-of-control locomotive. What's got you so upset?"

"Blue! They all brought something blue." She pressed her fisted hand to her chest. "Blue is *my* thing. What about old and new? Hasn't anybody ever heard about those?"

She stomped off to the bedroom, slamming that door, too. Herman gestured for the guys to leave. Jake, a little quicker to pick up on feminine moods, stood and headed for the door. Gus cupped his hands around his mouth and yelled, "I got news to cheer you up! They're starting the poker tournament on Friday because of so many entries."

The door creaked open and Lola peeked out. "Oh really, that *is* good news. I can show certain people how things are done."

The door closed again. A few minutes passed and Gus swallowed, turning to face Herman. "Did I sort of set up my own sweetie for a poker smackdown?"

There were only two people she could be upset with for bringing something blue. The same two women would be in the poker tournament, too. With it starting on Friday, they could now participate *and* attend the wedding. It would be a packed weekend, but at least his weekend would be less rough than Gus's. "No need to mention it. After all, Eunice probably forgot about the tournament."

Gus snorted. "I guess I'd better get it over with." He held out his hand to Herman, who shook it. "Been nice knowing you."

"Same here."

Chapter Twenty-Three

STILL INTENT ON gathering clues on Ron's disappearance, or possibly non-disappearance, Herman stared at the blank laptop screen for the second day in a row. Normally, he considered himself adept at finding information, but not the pro that Hannah, former librarian, was. She could find anything with a couple of keystrokes, even stuff people didn't want to be found—a much-needed skill for the senior sleuths, but one presently he couldn't access due to his beloved being upset with Hannah and Eunice for showing up with something blue before Lola did. In a way, he could see her beef. After all, she used a cane and their apartment took longer to reach than the others, being a coveted end unit with windows on two sides. Herman shrugged. Surely it would blow over soon, with the wedding on Saturday and today's poker tournament.

Singing came from the bedroom testifying to his wife's improved mood. At last, the skirmish ended and they'd be able to eat in the dining room with the other sleuths. His lips tipped up at the thought until he listened closely to the words—something about another one biting the dust. The bedroom door swung open and Lola emerged with a loud "Ta-dah!"

Throwing her arms high, she managed a slow three hundred and sixty degree turn without the aid of her cane. "What do you think?"

Herman started at her perfectly coiffed curls topped by a blue

LATE FOR THE WEDDING

fascinator with a bit of blue lace hanging onto her forehead. A chiffon dress with layers of tissue-thin blue fabric carried the color theme. Her navy ballet shoes, sky blue net gloves, and sapphire jewelry accessorized the outfit. So much blue made him blink. "I don't even recognize the dress."

"It's not mine," Lola confessed as she reached for her cane. "I borrowed it to make a point." She pointed a backward thumb at herself. "I'm the lady in blue, or better yet, the blue lady."

Obviously, the spat still festered, which didn't help his research at all. "Isn't the blue lady a ghost? A Story Inn ghost, which isn't too far from here?"

Her nose crinkled at his comment, making her huff. "Not the blue lady, then. Surely everyone will get my message."

"Oh," Herman drew out the word. "I have no doubt about that. What I really want to know is why it's so important? Isn't this a tiny bit childish?"

"Childish?" Lola repeated the word in a throaty rasp as she moved closer, drawing out a chair at the table. "Was it childish when Jake refused to speak to you for two weeks after you announced he dyed his hair to everyone within hearing distance?"

Before Herman could concur that it was indeed childish, Lola kept going. "What about how you and Gus battled for Ron's attention, jealous if he addressed one of you first as opposed to the other?"

"Hey, there…" Herman held up his hand, hoping to stop the many examples he knew would be coming. "As for Ron, it was the principle. Protocol, you might say. It made me feel as if I were back in the army."

"Okay." His wife held up the thumb on her right hand. "I'll give you that. Besides, the deal with blue was, according to folklore, blue represented good fortune. I wanted to wish Marcy luck in her marriage."

"Makes sense." Herman bobbed his head. "Don't you think everyone wants to wish Marcy and Lance well?"

"Of course." She placed her hand over her husband's and smiled. "You have a way of explaining things that makes sense. That's your superpower."

"It's not up there with flying or leaping a tall building."

Lola gave his hand a squeeze. "Maybe not, but it's much more needed." She released his hand and sighed. "I guess I need to change. Texas hold 'em is hard enough without dealing with net gloves and peering through a veil of lace."

The cane tapped lightly against the floor as Lola returned to the bedroom. Most of the residents and staff would pack themselves into the joined meeting hall between C and D Wings for the tournament. The sliding wall that separated the two rooms would be pushed back to create one gigantic room for functions such as this. Green tablecloths would cover the tables, their nod to felt. Staff members volunteered to be dealers to get out of their regular work. Herman heard a few even offered to be servers, but probably without the fishnet hose or short skirts. This meant foot traffic would be in the C and D Wings and not by the administration wing, which made it the perfect time to snoop. All the same, he didn't want to miss out on Lola's game.

He'd better check it out and plan accordingly. Herman knocked on the bedroom door and then opened it. "When's your time?"

"Two."

Herman glanced at his watch. "That's over an hour from now."

"True enough, but I need to be there for the rules, eye the other players, and throw in some trash talk." The last she admitted with a giggle.

"The good seats will go fast," Herman offered, eager to start his mission.

The layers of chiffon made whatever Lola said indecipherable as she wiggled out of the blue dress and threw it on the bed. "You're right," she finally said and reached for a rose-decorated blouse. "Good thing you convinced me to change. Now, I can wear my lucky blush pants suit."

Even though he'd seen his wife wear the outfit plenty of times, he never knew its lucky status. "What's so lucky about it?"

She tucked her blouse into her pants waistband and winked. "I wore it the day I met you."

How sweet she counted herself lucky to have met him. A step brought him to her side—the better to hug her. "I'm the lucky one. No matter what happens, we're both winners because we have each other."

"You're right," Lola whispered. "But I'm still going to beat the pants off those other players."

VOICES ECHOED DOWN the hallway as residents and staff alike hurried to view the tournament. The drapes pushed wide allowed sunlight to illuminate the rooms, along with the lamps intended to provide a homey feeling. The brightly lit interior made it easy to see anyone who shouldn't be behind the police tape. Herman's plan included nipping in, taking a few photos, and finding the one significant clue that would solve the case.

It could be that Ron knew about the threat. Maybe he left a coded message to both Herman and Gus. Only, the words tended to be the same every time. He'd ask if they'd kept watch and to report. Whatever happened occurred when they were out on the lawn talking about podcasts and chocolate cake for lunch. Someone turned off the cameras and planted the bomb. Maybe it served as a warning or was meant to take Ron out. What little he gathered from Lance and Marcy indicated no one had been in the office, which meant it served as a distraction to hustle Ron out. He'd almost swear he saw Ron's car leave along with the many other vehicles that exited.

No one believed he saw Ron. They said they did, but it felt as if he was being humored. All the same, if Ron never made it to work, wouldn't an explosion have cause him to show up? Lost in his musings, he peered down both hallways before ducking under the tape and pushing past a portable screen that maintenance had set up to protect the crime scene and give the agents investigating some privacy. It cut down on the rubberneckers, too.

He backed into the room, watching the empty hallway, and ready to drop down to tie a shoelace if someone should show. It was not the best excuse, but it would serve. The edge of his shirt wrapped around his hand allowed him not to leave any fingerprints at the scene. Holding his breath, he stepped backward and bumped into someone.

"Oh!" a feminine voice exclaimed.

His shoulders tensed and his stomach lurched as he turned, ready to shake out the confused senior excuse. "Oh, is this where the tournament is?"

To his surprise, Katie stood there, clutching long ledger-style books. "Oh, it's you," she replied in a breathy tone. One eyebrow went up as she said, "This isn't where the tournament is held and I believe you know as much. Uncle Jake told me how you seniors act confused to get out of trouble."

He covered his heart with his hand, feeling the betrayal. What else had he said? He would have sworn that Jake would be the most tight-lipped among them. Gus or Eunice saying something wouldn't have shocked him as much. "He did?"

"Yes, he did."

Well, so much for that tactic. Might as well go to the defensive. "What are *you* doing here?" It was hard to sound outraged when you couldn't raise your voice.

Being well versed in the art of debate by having a teenager, Katie lobbed it right back at him. "Why are *you* here?"

Never a fluent liar, or a believable one, Herman stuck to the truth as much as possible when that didn't work. "I cared about Ron. He's important to me."

"Me, too…" A catch sounded in Katie's voice.

Herman decided a full confession might be best since he hadn't done anything wrong. "I saw Ron on the day of the bombing and no one believes me. That receptionist swears he never even arrived, but I know better."

Katie's mouth dropped open and she gulped. "I know he was here, too. We were…" She glanced down at the floor before saying, "…friends."

It didn't take a rocket scientist to interpret that she wished they were much more. Vaguely uncomfortable with extracting information from a female on the verge of crying, Herman looked over his shoulder as if Marcy or Lance might enter the room and take over. No one waited by the screen. Herman cleared his throat. "How did you two become acquainted?"

Katie inhaled as if steeling herself. "Well, you know the director left immediately after Arnold's death."

Herman didn't know that but settled for a slow nod as if he did and not to interrupt.

"Arnold made it hard to do my work because he showed me very little and taught me less. When he died, bills came in that I didn't know if they'd been paid or not. A huge job of playing catch up. Weirdly, the day before he died, his computer went missing. I remember him using old ledgers, though." She held up the books in her hands. "I've been looking for these forever and I hope they help me to make sense of things because I can't lose my job. Ron helped me search. Arnold even carried the journals with him. The only time he didn't have them is when he left them with the director—the one person he *did* trust. That's why I thought they must be in here. They were tucked away under the carpet in the closet."

Sure, that's where every honest businessperson kept their financial ledgers. He pressed his lips together, wondering why the agents hadn't found them. Should she even have the ledgers, especially if embezzling might be happening? The more he heard, the less culpable it made Katie. Then again, it might be wishful thinking. He indicated the ledgers with his hand. "Shouldn't those be given to the agents? Scene of the crime? Evidence?"

Her arms tightened around the books. "I'd know what they mean. I could tell if it was legitimate or faked books."

"You still could by helping the authorities. Don't you want to help find Ron?" He knew she did and it might be the turning point. Lola did insist he could explain things in a way that made sense. "After all, you saw him that day."

"Not actually saw him…" She sniffed and glanced up, possibly to tamp back tears. "I brought him the patent leather shoes as a joke. You know, because he always shined his shoes. He told me once a real soldier would never be caught in patent leather. When I saw the shoes at the mall, I bought them, even though I knew they were the wrong size, just as a joke. They were still in the box in his office on his desk. After the bombing, I saw they were out of the box, lined up against the wall with not even a speck of dust on them, which I took as a sign."

The shoes he regarded as a clue, but maybe a little less once he figured out, they weren't Ron's shoes. He should have known better. A veteran wouldn't don patent leather. Blame it on Gus, who insisted they were Ron's shoes. "What message did the shoes give you?"

"That he's alive, of course!" She backhanded a tear. "I just don't know why I haven't heard from him."

Chapter Twenty-Four

GREENER PASTURES' WELL-LIT corridors were empty and quiet with the exception of some distant banging from the kitchen area. Those workers were slapping the food trays and the steam table pans with a little more force than necessary, upset that they didn't have the opportunity to attend the opening ceremonies of the Texas hold 'em tournament. Since they'd prepared the refreshments, they'd be familiar with the individual servings of pretzels and sugar cookies. The coffee, tea, and lemonade would appear in the poker room. The only thing missing would be actual dietary employees to serve.

That may not have been something the kitchen staff considered in their rush to get things done, Herman mused, as he watched Katie walk away with the ledger books. What if she didn't call the police? What if he didn't know Katie at all and she vanished, too? He fisted his hands and sucked in his lips—the next step in the case would depend on his doing the right thing. Too bad the right thing seldom arrived with a blinking neon sign to prompt appropriate action.

The baking chocolate aroma snaked out of the open dining room doors and wrapped itself around him, whispering of brownies and chocolate chip cookies. By the time he shook off the mouth-watering distraction, no one shared the corridor with him.

He'd been done in by a wayward sweet tooth—certainly nothing he'd want to confess. *Oh, and by the way, I may have solved the embezzling issue, but I allowed the evidence to stroll away.* Besides lambasting himself, what could he have done? He couldn't tackle Katie for the ledger books without damaging both his knees and his dignity. Katie could slap an assault charge on him, too. Tired of second-guessing himself, he decided to visit Katie's office. There was no way the woman could have disappeared in his momentary sugar-fueled daydream.

His rubber-soled shoes made a shushing noise that bore no resemblance to his rising frustration. No one ever suspected the clean-cut employee who never raised her voice and always said please and thank you. They're usually the killers when it isn't the grandmother who drives the bookmobile. A muscular twitch in his side had him wishing he could stop, but he soldiered on. After all, no one else could do what needed to be done. He checked the numbers and titles affixed to the offices. The best he could remember was Accounting butted up next to the PT office. Gus joked about Katie doing *financial heavy lifting.* At the time, the joke earned very few laughs, but what if she were fudging numbers and then blamed it on people who weren't there? There was no way anyone could prove otherwise.

When he finally reached the office, he could hear voices behind the closed door. He hesitated entering and held up his fist to knock because manners demanded it. He recognized the second voice and swung the door open, forgetting to knock. The woman bending over the ledger, turning the pages with latex gloves, glanced up.

"Marcy!" When he realized he'd practically shouted the name, relieved not to meet up with another possible suspect, he tried to cover it with a cough. In a much lower voice he said, "Good to see you."

"You saw me earlier," she pointed out and closed the ledger. She turned to address Katie. "A forensic accountant will need to go over this, but I'd like you to help since the forensic accountant will have no clue what's an actual account and what isn't."

"I'd be glad to help. You don't think I'll get in trouble for this?" She tucked a lock of hair behind her ear and winced.

"No reason you should unless your boss is dirty, and then he'll be the one in trouble," Marcy assured as she pushed the ledgers into a trash bag. "Not exactly evidence bag quality, but they're really big books."

"I'm not even sure who my boss is anymore, with Ron gone." She rested her hands behind her on the desk and exhaled hard. "I'm just glad Herman led me in the right direction. I think he already knew about the possible embezzlement."

"Oh really?" Marcy remarked, narrowing her eyes in Herman's direction. She held up her phone. "I'm calling for an evidence escort. If this is as important as I think it is, I can't take a chance of it getting lost from here to there."

As Marcy made her call, Katie busied herself around her office, possibly to pretend not to hear. Herman kept as still as possible, trying to deduce who she was talking to and if he fit into the conversation in any manner. He'd rather his name didn't come up. Marcy pulled the phone away from her ear. "Anything else I might need to know that you may have forgotten to mention?"

Was she mad? It was hard to say, but a person less generous than himself might call her tone testy. As a bride, nerves grew frazzled, turning normal women into demanding divas nicknamed *bridezil-las*. He'd not slap that label on her. "Could you tell Lance that Cleo is actually a name from a podcast and not a murderer? Well, she *might* be a murderer. I didn't listen to the podcast, but if she is a murderer, it has nothing to do with the current case."

"Good to know." She gave a short nod and glanced at her phone. "I need to wait on pickup, but I promised Lola I'd be there for her opening game. It's about to start."

"Oh my!" He turned to the door, ready to move and well aware his first priority should be supporting his beloved. Marcy continued to speak.

"Tell her I'll get there as soon as possible. Also, tell her she did herself proud." She waited until Herman nodded and then added, "I'll see all of you at the wedding tomorrow. So much to do before I say, 'I do.'"

"I bet," Herman acknowledged, waved, and speed walked to the tournament, hoping his beloved wouldn't have to play against anyone she called *friend*.

Chapter Twenty-Five

LAUGHTER AND CLAPPING spilled from the tournament room as Herman approached it. The hallway narrowed and somehow lengthened, making it more distant. The lights blinked, or did they? Despite his desire to reach the room before Lola sat down to play, his destination kept moving—not unlike the case. What he thought he knew turned out to be questionable. A ringing in his ears and a sudden temperature spike forced him to the wall for support. He breathed slowly and closed his eyes, trying to find the happy place the Internet meditation guru suggested. Instead of tropical blue waters and a sandy beach, he found himself seated around a table with the fellow sleuths, brainstorming—that was his happy place. Maybe the race mattered much more than the finish line.

"Herman, are you all right?" a female voice inquired nearby, forcing him to open his eyes to Hannah's concerned expression. "I am now." The ear ringing lessened and the hall no longer kept extending. Herman used his sleeve to wipe away the cold sweat and wiggled his shoulders, shaking off any lingering effects from almost fainting. "I guess I thought I needed to solve the bombing on my own and became overwhelmed when I realized I was going nowhere fast."

"Well, that's stinky thinking." She patted his arm. "You do realize the cold cases we solved had already been handled by professionals, and their data was fed into computers used to profile individuals—and still they remained unsolved?"

Sometimes, he considered Hannah to be one of the smartest of the sleuths, but today, she wasn't making any sense. "How'd we solve them, then?"

"Right place, right time, and obviously, the right people." She chuckled, smirked, and poked Herman until he grinned, too. "Consider that years pass, things change, and then one of us questions someone who knew the victim or even witnessed the crime. I like to think of all of us as non-confrontational, with the exception of Eunice, of course. Her feistiness works for her, though. Anyhow, a person doesn't feel intimidated talking to us. With the police, they keep their mouths shut, not wanting to get themselves involved in the case. That's one reason we solve cases—not to mention perseverance. This bombing might never be solved, and we have to be okay with that."

Herman nodded at the explanation. It was meant to soothe, but he mentally vowed not to give up on the case. If he could help the ATF agents in any way, he would. The announcer introduced the next players, including Lola. "I need to go inside."

"I understand."

They both squeezed into the packed room, breathing in the scent of coffee mingled with Old Spice cologne and floral perfumes. Some experts declared the sense of smell lessened first, while others declared it stayed strong until the end. In Herman's opinion, it had to be the latter. Along with the coffee and cologne, he could identify muscle rub, cookies, and that awful deodorizer scent under everything. Strange, he hadn't been able to detect the coppery scent of blood on the blotter. Obviously, his sniffer still worked, but he'd never replace a bloodhound.

A smattering of applause drew him to the main table where the women players had arrived. One sported sunglasses to prevent anyone judging the content of her cards from her eyes. In Texas hold 'em, there were five community cards that the dealer dealt upright, while each player received two hole cards that were dealt down. More likely, the player would struggle to see her own cards with the shades on.

His beautiful bride arrived all smiles, waving to everyone and looking confident. When she spotted Herman, she blew him a kiss, causing a few *ahs*. The emcee reminded the audience they needed to be quiet to allow the players to concentrate. As soon as he said that, he heard someone yell, "What did he say?"

Fortunately for his bride, she could concentrate in a crowded casino. This should be nothing for her. However, for him, it turned into the longest sixty minutes ever as he shifted his weight from foot to foot and finally settled for holding up a wall.

"Alrighty, folks," the announcer said as Lola revealed her cards. "We have a winner. No surprise this game goes to our own lovely Vegas transplant."

Clapping erupted, a few cheers were heard, and Herman added, "Way to go, Lola!"

She stood, took a few bows, and made her way toward Herman slowly, accepting the congratulations of various members. While some were certainly rooting against her, everyone loved a winner.

"I knew you'd win," Herman said and leaned down to kiss his bride.

"Thanks, sweetie." She covered his hand with her own and gave it a squeeze. "The first game didn't present too many challenges. Throw in a couple of one armed bandits dinging away and cigarette smoke, and it would feel like Vegas." Her lips drew up in a flirtatious moue. "Or at least Reno."

"First game?" Even though he knew what the words symbolized, Herman repeated them in hopes he'd be told otherwise.

"Yes." Her forehead furrowed and she cocked her head. "Did you think there was only one game?"

To admit this would sound silly—Herman chose to backpedal. "I thought there'd be several games going on at the same time."

"I think that was the original plan. They started out with three or four tables in the beginning, but it got confusing—at least for the participants, who complained the emcee soured their game. That's why we're down to one table and the call for silence."

He was not a math whiz, but Herman knew the tournament would linger forever like a bad head cold. "Will you play again today?"

"There's a good chance."

"So, you wouldn't want to step out for a bit of fresh air, would you?" The thought appealed to him.

"Oh, no." She gave her head an emphatic shake. "I need to size up the players. I know this is boring to you, but I appreciate your indulging me. You go do something fun. Maybe you can bring me dinner in case they don't deliver food to the tournament players. Something light. I can't worry about acid reflux and be at my best at the same time."

"Can do," he promised as Lola gave him an affectionate pat and drifted back into the crowd. He watched his wife blend in with her well-wishers and considered what would be fun and, at the same time, give him a chance to stop by a fast-food restaurant. Maybe he should drive by Ron's house and take a little looksee—but to do that, he'd need an address. Fortunately, he knew just the person to ask.

Chapter Twenty-Six

THE SOUND OF the tournament dwindled to a tinny echo. Then again, it still might be his ears ringing. Herman boxed one ear, then the other, earning an odd look from a passing resident. Not knowing how to explain his actions, he grumbled, "It's murder getting old."

"Don't I know it," the walker replied.

Herman picked up his steps, anxious to put his plan into action. As far as getting old, as long as he could drive and lend a hand solving mysteries, he participated in more worthwhile adventures than he did ten years ago. Best of all, he'd somehow, against all odds, landed the belle of the center. That still puzzled him.

Another turn brought him to Katie, who sat inside her office, working her way through a tissue box. Ah, a weepy female, the most unpredictable of creatures. Whatever he might say would be wrong and turn the waterworks even higher. *Be brave.* The clue he could retrieve might change the entire case. Herman inhaled, straightened his shoulders, and marched inside. "Hello, Katie. I'm glad to see you're feeling better."

Red-rimmed eyes stared up at him. "I'm *not* feeling better." The wadded-up tissue served to dab at her eyes.

It was not the lead-in he wanted. He shuffled his feet and glanced at the floor. As a gentleman, he should commiserate with her, but he didn't have all day. If he expected to get a look at Ron's house and swing back by the fish shack, he'd better get moving. "Sorry about that. Could I have Ron's address?"

The last part he said so fast that she might not have understood if the dumbfounded expression, including the gaping mouth, were any indication. She shut it with a snap and then asked as she stood, "You want Ron's address?"

It sounded rhetorical, but to be safe, Herman answered. "Yes, I do. I would appreciate it right away, too."

Katie slowly walked around Herman, eyeing him as she did. A hand sneaked up on her hip and she asked, "Why do you want his address?"

"To visit him, of course."

She pressed her lips together as if giving the matter weighty thought. "All right, I'll give you his address. It will even be the current one, if I come along."

"Will you be crying every mile or so?" It was a bit on the rude side, but he knew his limits. He didn't drive crying women around if he could help it.

Katie sniffed, wiped her eyes, and announced, "I can do it," with a bit of a tremble. "I promise not to cry. Besides, I gave the agents his old address."

"Katie!" His eyes widened at the implication. "That might earn you an obstruction of justice or some other such crime."

"Maybe." She jerked up her chin. "I don't care. I thought I might be protecting Ron. Shouldn't they be able to look up his address on their computers?"

"I guess. Sure, they'll be using the same Internet as everyone else. Speaking of that," Herman remembered what he never had an opportunity to check out, "is your computer up?"

"It is."

"Could I look up a name before we leave?"

Katie gestured to the open laptop on her desk. "Be my guest. What are you looking for?"

Normally, he kept the details of the cold cases to himself. However, the current case rated neither cold nor his, plus Katie's sadness tore at him. He strolled to the desk and sat in the rolling desk chair. He clicked on the search engine and carefully typed out *Stacey Reuben*. A list with several hits came up. Sometimes, the same person got several mentions. There was no story about a much-decorated veteran dying in combat. "This is no help at all."

"What's no help?" Katie skirted the desk and read the screen. "Who's Stacey Reuben?"

"I'm not sure. Never met him as far as I can remember."

"Let's try this." She leaned over the desk and swiveled the computer in her direction. "Sometimes, if I can't put a name and a face together, I try to pull up a picture." She clicked on images and typed the name in—a series of faces appeared, including both male and female. Some were selfies, but others were group shots. What a mess. Herman stared at the images and mumbled, "None of them look the least bit familiar."

"There are several pages. Let's try another one. The farther you go the less likely you'll be able to get a photo with the right name." She clicked on the arrow button and brought up more unknown faces.

Nothing—a few middle-aged women with less than flattering haircuts, a doodle-type dog apparently named Stacey, and a youngster still in short pants who must have shared the name. Near the edge of the page, an unsmiling man in fatigues with a buzz haircut stared out at them. Katie's index finger touched the photo. "That could be Ron's twin." She uttered the words in almost a whisper.

"There's *some* similarity. No scar, though. This man is possibly a decade younger than Ron. Sometimes, folks just look alike."

"No," she gave a little sniff, cleared her throat, and firmed up her voice. "It's him. I know it's him. Look at the eyes. It could be an old photo when he was younger and before he got the scar."

"And before he started calling himself Ron, too. Now we definitely have to check out the house."

Grabbing a piece of paper and a pen, Katie changed screens to a series of addresses and wrote one down. Apparently, Herman guessed wrong when he imagined Katie and Ron might be better acquainted since she insisted the shoes weren't his size. Perhaps a relationship between the two did exist. Ron, or whatever he went by, may have encouraged the relationship, hoping it might prove beneficial.

The two wasted no time walking to the parking lot. Once in the car, Katie proved herself to be a more opinionated passenger than either Gus or Jake.

"Can't you go any faster?"

"I could, but I'd get a ticket." Why people thought you could speed everywhere puzzled him. Since he'd heard complaints about his driving before, he shook it off. "Not sure why we're rushing around. I doubt we'll find anyone at the house."

"You're probably right." Katie stared out the side window, not speaking for several minutes as Herman drove. After several cars passed Herman with the last one earning a beep for its closeness, Katie finally spoke. "I thought he really liked me."

"He may have. He could have. I'm not saying he didn't." Not sure if he'd made himself clear, Herman added, "A lot of villains have good traits, such as they love animals or possess artistic talent."

"Yeah." A derisive snort expressed how she felt about it. "Maybe I'm not the best at picking out men. I'll give you that." A heavy sigh escaped and then silence ensued.

He was not the lady's man Jake considered himself to be, but Herman knew one thing about dealing with uncomfortable situations, although he didn't always use it. When nothing positive could be said, it was best to say nothing. He drove with Katie making indecipherable mutters, which could have served as directions or recriminations for falling for someone who failed to live up to the image, she'd spun for him.

A sign bookended by stone lions declared the neighborhood to be *Tranquil Manor*—an odd name for the older brick ranch homes with modest yards. Herman slowed even more as he read the house numbers. Many were sun-faded or missing a number, making it nearly impossible for a delivery driver or someone intent on snooping.

Ron's house came into view with all its numbers. Leaves littered the yard around the empty driveway. Herman slowed to a stop directly opposite the house and parked. "You say Ron mentioned moving? Did he give a reason why?"

"No." Katie's hand rested on the door handle as she made ready to spring from the car. She looked ready to hammer on the door and demand that Ron or whoever answer. "I didn't realize I should ask. He told me recently—even gave me the address. I put it in my computer so I wouldn't misplace the paper." She gasped and then let go of the door to press her hand to her heart.

"What is it?" Herman asked, alarm flooding his body and creating a desire to flee the situation. "Heart attack? Should I call 911?"

"No! Don't call 911." Her face scrunched up as she bit her lip. "I think Ron or Stacey tried to give me a clue or something."

Momentary alarm drifted away, allowing Herman to breathe easier, replaced with creeping excitement. "How so?"

"He told me there was no need to change the address in the personnel files, but he wanted me to have it."

"Sounds suspicious."

"It means he cares." Katie crossed her arms over her chest as if giving herself a hug. While Ron's peculiar behavior raised several questions, he wouldn't rate it as a declaration of love, in his opinion. "He must have trusted you. After all, he told you where the ledgers were."

"Oh, no. I worked that out on my own as I ducked into the closet to hide when I heard people coming. I recognized the feel of loose carpeting. We used to have loose boards that covered my secret place in my childhood home. I used to hide things from my brother. Naturally, I pulled up the carpet and there they waited—not stored in a protective case, either. Rather like someone just threw them in there in a hurry. At least I kept my candy in an old metal tin."

Herman damped a finger and ran it over his bushy brows. "You know we'll have to call and tell Marcy this."

"You're right," Katie agreed, shouldering her purse and placing her hand back on the door handle. "Why can't we have a looksee first without touching anything?"

"I wouldn't have it any other way."

They both got out in unison, but Herman turned and reached into the car for a magazine he kept in the car for such purposes. He wiggled the AARP magazine and confided in a low voice from a distance, "People think it's a religious tract and usually vanish when they see me coming."

"Very cool," Katie acknowledged and continued to cross the street.

Younger, more agile joints created a hardship for Herman as far as keeping pace. Fortunately, the distance between the car and house measured in yards, not miles. Katie stood staring into the front window, obvious to anyone who stepped out of their house or peered through curtains.

"Katie!" he hissed and motioned for her to follow him around the house to the back yard, complete with a privacy fence. Not too surprisingly, it had been bolted from the other side. The normal amount of jiggling failed to open it.

"Wait," Katie whispered, pawing through her purse. "I may have just the thing." A heavy brass letter opener appeared along with Katie's grin. "I can do this." She inserted the opener in the narrow slot between the fence and gate and worked it upward. When the gate refused to open, she instructed Herman. "I need you to hold the gate handle and lift it upward as I do this."

This forced Katie to scrunch down to work under Herman's arms. A few grunts later and the gate swung open. Once in, they closed the gate and found the lock to be barely hanging on, which made their entrance not such a big deal. Herman pulled out his camera and took a photo, wincing as he remembered holding onto the handle. "My fingerprints are on the handle and I have a feeling we aren't the first to enter without an invitation."

"Makes you wonder," Katie replied as she checked out the patchy lawn with a few plastic chairs knocked askew. "All I saw inside was a sofa and a side chair. No photos. No rugs or lamps. Not much of anything."

"Most bachelors aren't big on fixing up a place." Still, Herman's old home in North Carolina wouldn't fit the bachelor stereotype. "Maybe he didn't have time."

"Maybe," Katie confirmed as she headed to an unattached garage that sat inside the fence.

Weird. Most of the other houses boasted attached garages—this must have been a later addition. If his car resided inside, it would answer the question of what happened to the car. While everyone rushed out of the building, the fake Ron jumped into his car and drove home.

"Anything?" Herman asked as he joined Katie at the side garage window.

"Nothing. No car. He keeps a clean garage. Some stuff on a work table, but that's it."

Herman moved closer to the window but refused to repeat his earlier mistake by touching it. The insides were oddly empty of garden tools, boxes, and most importantly, vehicles. Still, he sniffed and recognized the heavy scent of motor oil. There were no cars and no oil stains—not even a shelf full of car additives to account for the stench. *Odd.*

Then he remembered. Gus mentioned the gray smoke streaming from the building indicated high explosives—possibly military-grade C-4, which smelled like motor oil. On the workbench were wires and wire snips. An uneasy feeling tapped him on the shoulder, and he reached for Katie's arm. "We need to get out of here now!"

"What?" She resisted, pulling against his grasp. "We just got here and haven't found out anything useful. Shouldn't we stay until we find something of value?"

"We just did. Ron made the bomb. It may not have been the only bomb, either. I got a gut feeling that's telling me to run like the wind. Whenever I get that feeling, I listen, which is why I have survived to be as old as I am."

Without another word, they both sprinted out the gate, leaving it unlatched, and into the car. Herman twisted the key into the ignition. Once the engine roared to life, his left hand tighten on the steering wheel as he pushed the gear shift into drive, and stepped on the gas. The sudden movement jerked the occupants forward, then slapped them back against the seats. An explosion erupting in the area they'd so recently abandoned, resulted in Herman stomping on the brake and squealing the tires as the sedan shuddered to a stop. Once again, both Katie and Herman's bodies jerked forward again as if crash test dummies.

Katie grabbed at her shoulder restrain and pulled it away from her neck exposing a red welt. "Good thing, I put on my seat belt. Instead of a belt mark, I could be picking up my teeth from the dashboard."

"Good thing," Herman agreed as he weighed his options. Explosions could be a calling card of a nefarious sort. It didn't matter if he just happened to be sneaking around without telling anyone. Afterall, it would be hard to overlook an explosion. Someone would call it in—it might as well be him. "We need to call police now! I hope Marcy doesn't find out. It might put a damper on the wedding."

Chapter Twenty-Seven

EMERGENCY VEHICLES' LIGHTS flashed and radio chatter ensued as the police and firefighters stared at the pile of broken lumber and crumbled concrete blocks that used to be a garage. Neighbors gathered on their front stoops in the formerly quiet neighborhood. One elderly woman flagged down Marcy.

"Excuse me, are you important?"

Since it happened to be the first time someone asked such a bold question, she hesitated before answering. "I'm a detective, if that helps determine my importance."

"Good enough," the woman decided. "I saw two suspicious people creeping around right before the explosion."

Herman, who'd parked his car and snuck back to see the results of the explosion, swallowed hard when he spotted the woman detaining Marcy. You'd think the soon to be bride could have taken the day off and had her nails done for the upcoming wedding. It probably didn't help he called her to report the explosion. A trellis supporting a heart-shaped leaf vining plant hid him but perhaps not well.

The woman chatting with Marcy pointed in his direction and shouted, "There he is!" which caused everyone to stare directly at him. Lurking in the shadows only emphasized guilt, but he stayed until Marcy beckoned. As he moved closer, he heard the good detective explain. "I believe this gentleman is the one who called the police. Excuse me, sir?" She turned slightly and addressed Herman. "Aren't you the one who called?"

"Yes, I am." He recognized the rescue ring Marcy had tossed him. "Myself and another associate were out distributing church literature."

The nosy neighbor wrinkled her nose and focused on picking lint off her sweater. She glanced up, catching Herman's scrutiny. "You didn't need to go around the back to do so."

"Actually, I do." Herman regarded her with a serious mien. "You may find this hard to believe, but some people ignore us when we come to the front door. Like the old saying, *backdoor friends are the best*, we're just trying to start out as friends."

"Hmmpf!" Her reaction demonstrated her disbelief. "After all that nosing around, you two sure flew out of there."

Good thing they did or they'd be history. Even though Marcy worked hard to hide her smile, Herman sensed she enjoyed his discomfort. He probably thought it suited him since he went sneaking around without permission. What would make a door-to-door salesperson hit the road in a hurry? "I thought I heard a dog."

"Possible," the woman allowed. "Plenty of dogs in the neighborhood. None of them are too big, though. Certainly not large enough for you to run as fast as you did."

"I'm very afraid of dogs," he admitted and then glanced down at his toes as if shamed by the fact.

Perhaps Marcy felt he'd suffered enough as she thanked the woman and asked her to return to her porch. Once she'd judged the nosy Nellie couldn't eavesdrop, she said, "Okay, spill."

"You know I'm worried about Ron. No one else seems all that concerned. Katie is worried, too."

"You brought someone into your unsanctioned sleuthing?" She crossed her arms and narrowed her eyes.

Somehow, he had consistently upset every woman he met today with the exception of his beloved. Most of her happiness probably had to do with winning at poker. "Ah, not exactly. I happened to ask what Ron's address was when I left to go get something for Lola's supper. I need to go get her dinner before it's her time to play."

"Your running to pick up fast food is somehow connected to a garage exploding?" She blew out a breath, ruffling her bangs.

"Well, Katie explained to me that Ron didn't want anyone to know he'd moved, except her. He's sweet on Katie, or at least that's what he wants Katie to believe."

"Yeah, there's something up with the two of them. By the way, where *is* Katie?"

"In the car." Herman gestured behind him as if the car were feet away as opposed to a couple of blocks.

"I hope so. She could easily take the car and run. After all, you mentioned…" She held up her right hand with her index and middle finger entwined. "…they were like this."

"Not exactly. Given time, maybe." He glanced at his watch. "I need to be getting back to the center."

"That part I agree with." She dipped her head and asked, "What did you see that had you running, especially with your knees?"

"Back when the explosion happened at the center, there was dirty gray smoke that Gus identified as C-4. It also smells like motor oil."

"I'm familiar with it. Continue."

"Anyhow, I peered through the garage window and noticed everything was all clean. No car. No garden supplies. Nothing except for the smell of motor oil and wires and a wire cutter on the workbench. Something told me to run, so I did. I dragged Katie along with me."

Another vehicle pulled up and dark-suited agents climbed out. Marcy acknowledged them with a wave and then nudged Herman. "Go now and get Lola her dinner. The agents will want to talk to you later."

"They know where to find me," Herman offered and then hustled toward his car, limping a little. With his luck, he had pulled something due to having not run for at least a decade or two.

Back in the car, which thankfully stayed where he had left it, a tearful Katie cradled her phone as if it were a kitten or a winning lottery ticket. The younger set certainly cherished their phones. He started the car and tried not to look at Katie since he'd need to make an inquiry about her teary state or offer something comforting. Quite frankly, he could do neither at the present time. Instead, he drove to the nearest fast-food restaurant, unaware of how much time had passed between the explosion and now. Knowing a Jolly burger and fries never earned the title of something light, Herman made sure to add a strawberry milkshake. Surely that should please.

Thankfully, the entire trip back, Katie neither cried nor talked—possibly traumatized by the explosion. With two under his belt, it should be getting old hat, but perhaps not for Katie. "We're almost there," he offered in a soft voice. "Are you okay?"

"I'm more than okay." She spoke in a breathy manner more suited to a preteen girl gushing about her boy band idol. Herman turned, catching a glimpse of Katie's trembling smile.

"What's put you in such a good mood?" Another example of why women baffled men.

"He called."

"Who?" he asked, even though he had an inkling of who might cause such a reaction.

"You know. Ron."

"Did he identify as Ron?"

"He didn't have to. I recognized his voice. He's okay."

"That's dandy." Even though he considered himself to be mellow, a bit of a sneer sounded in his voice. Why not? Hadn't he done everything in his power to help find the man? Did *he* get a call? Nope. "Did he explain about the bombing?"

"Which one?"

"Any of them."

"No. But he will. He just needs time."

Herman pulled into the parking lot and noticed some thoughtless individual had parked in his space, which forced him to park elsewhere. He grabbed the bag of food and the shake and settled into what he labeled his *stern look*. "You need to call the police and tell them Ron called you. It's important."

"I will." She opened the door and stepped out. "I'd like to get back to my office for a little privacy. Wish Lola good luck for me."

"Will do." Part of him wanted to follow her and prompt her to call, rather like an annoying sheepdog. Instead of herding sheep, he reminded people what they needed to do. Both Jake and Gus pointed out this tendency. His wife may have also mentioned it in passing. Right now, food delivery served as his first priority, and then he could munch down on the double Jolly burger and loaded fries he got for himself.

Chapter Twenty-Eight

THE MORNING OF the wedding arrived with heavy ground fog. Herman winced as he considered driving somewhere new and into another state in such weather. "I don't like the looks of this."

Yawning, Lola moved to stand beside him. "Just fog. It will burn off by ten."

"We need to be there *by* ten. The wedding is at one."

Lola leaned her head on Herman's shoulder. "Remember when we drove down to North Carolina so I could meet your friends?"

"I do." Herman sensed where she might be going, but all the same pretended otherwise.

"You had no issues on *that* trip."

Actually, he had, but none he'd mentioned. As long as his beloved had enjoyed the pastoral scenes, she'd not seen his confusion at renumbered exits due to extending the highway. There were times he resorted to the GPS on his phone. "I wanted to impress you. Show I could take care of you."

"You'd already impressed me. After all, we were engaged." She lifted her head and gave him a little pat. "Besides, I'm sure the fog is localized due to all the bodies of water nearby. It should have lifted by the time we leave. Anyway, need to get my special events face on."

"What?" It sounded like she said *special events face.*

Lola chuckled as she weaved her way to the bedroom by touching the furniture for balance. "You men! I have to really doll up for the wedding."

"Okay." At least that much he understood. "I'll make some coffee and toast since the dining room won't be open for another hour. The drive should take two hours, but we need to give ourselves plenty of buffer time—not knowing what the traffic is and all. Lance is picking up Gus and Jake. Marcy is riding with Hannah, so the groom doesn't see her before the ceremony."

Lola called over her shoulder as she opened the bedroom door. "Oh, I heard. Originally, Eunice was supposed to ride with us, but she shoehorned herself into the bride car, as she called it."

Thinking of the previous trips he'd taken with Eunice, Herman pressed a hand against his chest and smirked. "Oh, the hardship, not to have her constant driving directions."

"No worries, she'll be coming back with us."

"Lucky us. I imagine Gus will, too."

"Probably," Lola concurred. "That way Hannah and Jake can ride together. So romantic, right after the wedding. Who knows what might occur?"

"Jake snoring the entire way back?"

"You could be right." Lola disappeared into the bedroom and Herman set about making breakfast.

ABOUT AN HOUR later, the sleuths met him in the parking lot, ready for their wedding convoy minus the armed guards, unless Marcy or Lance had hidden a gun in their wedding finery. Most of the fog had lifted, but a few pockets remained here and there. Gus sidled up to both Herman and Jake with a large opaque plastic bag that he rattled. It emitted a metallic clanging. It sounded like trouble, but Herman asked anyhow. "What's in the bag?"

"The best I could do as far as putting a shivaree together with as little time as we had."

"Shivaree?" Jake said. "I thought that custom went out years ago."

"Not yet." Gus shook his bag, demonstrating his intent. "That's the problem with people today, they don't know how to have fun."

The word shivaree reminded him of the old musical, *Oklahoma!* where at the end, the townspeople surrounded the honeymooners' house, banging on pots and pans, and shooting guns to celebrate the marriage. "You'd better not have any guns in there."

"Not actual guns. My grandson located some of my old cap pistols in a box in the attic. He even found a roll of cap paper. Not sure if it works, though."

Herman held out his hand for the bag. "Why don't I hold onto it? That way it will be a bigger surprise for the couple."

At the suggestion, Gus clutched the bag tighter, paced a few steps to the right, then the left, and finally returned to his original spot. He cleared his throat, holding out the bag. "Be careful, it's literally a party in a bag. There's noisemakers, poppers, cans, and streamers to tie onto the car, plus smoke bombs."

"Smoke bombs?" Jake crinkled his nose. "Why would we need those?"

"Fun. I thought I'd throw them in," Gus said as if it were self-evident. "Even put in a couple of lighters. What good is a smoke bomb without a way to light it?"

The mention of smoke bombs with an emphasis on *bomb* had Herman searching for Katie's car. Sometimes, she worked on Saturdays but not always. In last night's rush to deliver Lola's dinner and the second poker round, which his sweetie aced, he forgot to check if she'd notified the authorities about Ron's call. Sure, he could ask Marcy if Katie called and ruin the joyous wedding atmosphere. "Jake, is your niece working today?"

"I saw her in the office. Didn't stop to chat, worried I'd be late. Why do you ask?"

"Oh, I have a question for her."

"All right." Jake pulled out his phone, tapped in a number and spoke. "Herman has a question for you. Could you meet us in the front parking lot?" He listened and then laughed. "Yeah, I'll be the good-looking one. Love you, too. Bye." He pocketed the phone. "She'll be a couple of minutes—someone is in her office." Jake's brows pulled together as he mused aloud. "She said, 'Love you, Uncle Jake.' It's not like she's never said it before but never at the end of a call. Weird."

Lance arrived first, pulled up near the group, and powered down his window with a wide grin. "I've got to be at the chapel on time. Jump in, whoever is going with me."

Both Gus and Jake sprinted for the passenger side door, but Jake's longer legs served him. Surprisingly, he opened the door and allowed Gus to ride upfront.

Shocked at the out-of-the-ordinary display of good manners between the two, Lola caught Herman's eye and said, "I have a feeling this will be a day of miraculous events."

While most people would find the sentiment charming, it worried Herman. For a miracle to happen, usually something bad preceded it. If a person experienced miraculous healing, the individual must be sick or dying for it to happen. "I'll settle for happy, everyday occurrences."

"You're in luck." Lola wrapped her hand around her husband's arm. "I talked to the activity director, explained we were going to a wedding and she arranged my next game for later today. We'll be back in time to play."

"Should I ask if Hannah and Eunice are finalists?" His stomach turned when he realized the friends playing friends scenario still existed.

"Unfortunately, yes. They must have had unskilled opponents or plain luck."

Once the boys buckled up, Lance honked his horn and off they went. Everyone else waved, but Eunice fussed as she did so. "Where is Hannah? Everyone knows the bride needs more time than the groom to get ready."

"Don't worry. Hannah has a lead foot," Lola reminded. While this may have eased Eunice's nerves, it worried Herman.

"Remind me not to let you ride with Lead-Foot Hannah anymore."

"Don't be silly," Lola simpered at her husband, as a familiar compact turned into the parking lot. A white panel van pulled in after it. Hannah drove up to the waiting three and gave a spritely honk. Not needing to be told twice, Eunice grabbed hold of the back door, opened it, and music spilled out about *lighting up my life*. Not waiting to be asked, Eunice squeezed in beside a stack of gift wrapped boxes.

As they left, Lola nudged her husband. "Look at the white panel van. No lettering. Practically shouts *serial killer*."

Every crime drama featured a plain white van in their episodes—sometimes new, other times rust pocked, but always without back or side windows like this one. "Now who's being silly?"

The van idled in front of the center while a muscular man attired in black slid out and headed for the front doors. If they left now, they'd be only minutes behind the wedding party. Even so, Herman turned back to study the man who'd struck him as familiar. As the man entered the building, Herman remembered with a gulp. "I don't have a good feeling about this. We need to wait."

The two of them stood staring at the doors until Lola nudged her husband. "Katie never came out to answer your question."

The bad feeling that started out as the size of an apple grew to watermelon size, almost choking him. "We'd better get out of the open. Let's get in the car."

Herman assisted his wife into the sedan, handed her the shivaree bag, and then jogged to the other side and climbed in. As a precaution, he started the car in case they needed to leave fast.

"What is it about the man in the van that makes you nervous?" his wife asked, her voice going tight on the last word.

"I saw him give the receptionist an envelope."

Lola scratched her head and sniffed. "What's so bad about an envelope? It could be a payment or a note for a resident. Sounds more like something sweet."

"Not sweet. You weren't there. Have you ever seen the receptionist's face?"

"No, come to think of it."

"Me, either, until then." He pushed his hand through his hair. "She acted all animated and maybe a trifle scared, too. He put the envelope on the desk all secret-like and then she covered it with her hand and slid it off the desk. When they thought I might be watching, the man swung around when the receptionist almost took my head off. I blathered something about not being able to see well when I came in from the outside, which I think they accepted. Talk about dead eyes." He whistled. "I've seen folks with cold eyes, but nothing compared to this guy."

Instead of answering with one of her Vegas tales about run-ins with the mob, Lola remained focused on the center's front path where Katie walked between the receptionist and the dead eye guy. "I don't think she wants to be with them."

The panel truck's sliding door opened from inside and a man reached out to grab Katie as she struggled to get away from her escorts. For a brief second, her frightened eyes connected with Herman's before a final shove landed her inside the van. The side door slammed shut and both the receptionist and Dead Eyes climbed into the van.

Lola pointed to the van. "Don't lose it!"

Chapter Twenty-Nine

T HE VAN'S TIRES screeched as it tore out of the parking lot at high speed. Herman's knuckles whitened as he tightened his grip on the steering wheel to follow the van. "Lola, call the police!"

His bride clutched the phone, alternating between watching the action and offering unsolicited advice rather than actually calling. "Hurry up! They're getting away."

"They're crazy drivers." To demonstrate the fact, the kidnappers bumped over a median into oncoming traffic that honked and swerved to avoid the van. It took precious seconds for Herman to find an acceptable cut-through and make a legal U-turn. The van's catapult into the lane resulted in being turned sideways. Unless the driver barreled through the guard rail and slid down the hill, he'd end up making a three-point turn, irritating motorists in the process.

"Look at that!" Herman yelled while Lola pressed the call button, causing the phone to ring. "Who does that?"

"Criminals," Lola responded. A voice sounded on the phone. "Hello! I want to report a kidnapping in progress." A pause, then, "So sorry. Ignore the call, please."

"Wrong number?" Herman asked, keeping his eyes on the van that started picking up speed again. "We're really going to need some help of the professional variety."

"You're so right." She tapped at her phone again. "Police?" she questioned before launching into her tale. "My husband and I just witnessed a kidnapping at Greener Pastures Assisted Living Center. A man and the center's receptionist pushed Katie into a white panel van against her will."

Lola listened for a while. "No, it's not some pretend ambush getaway." A huff announced her disgust that such a thing would be suggested. "It has to do with the bombing and embezzling going on at the Greener Pastures. There should be some ATF Agents on the case in the vicinity. We're following the van now. License number?" She glanced at her husband.

"No license plate. They have a paper for a license that reads *tags are in the mail*."

"No plate," Lola answered. "I'm sure that does make it harder, but we're following them now and you could easily nab them for reckless driving and speeding, among a few other things."

Herman jerked the wheel and then jerked it back to stay on the road. "Squirrel."

"Road?" Lola repeated, craning her neck to see the sights. "Baxter Avenue. Herman," she asked," which way are we heading?"

"North. There's a light coming up and a whole bunch of cars stopped. Let's see what he does." The van pulled up behind another white panel van so much alike they could be twins, except the first one did have a license plate. This display of road etiquette baffled Herman, but before he could point it out, the car door slammed and Lola strolled around the hood of the car, keeping her hand on the car for balance. Once she reached the driver's side, she pulled it open.

"Switch places. I'm the faster driver. You handle the phone."

Herman hesitated. "Do you even have a license?"

"Of course I do. Now move!"

Herman stepped out, moved up the seat and helped Lola in, and then closed the door. The light turned green and, half-afraid that Lola would leave him, he jumped into the back seat, taking no chances. It was a good thing he did because Lola floored it once they were clear of traffic. To think he'd worried about Hannah's driving. The phone bounced around in the front seat with a disembodied voice calling out, "What's happening?"

Knowing he'd never catch the phone with Lola's wild moves, he called on his own cell. "Hello, police? I'm following up on the kidnapping. I can't reach my wife's phone."

Herman held the phone up to his ear while leaning forward to watch the van. At one point, the kidnappers' van pulled up onto the shoulder to cut around the other white van. "Oh no!"

"Sir? Sir, what road are you on?" a dispatcher yelled to get Herman's attention.

"Mount Tabor. Cross street Grant Line."

Lola laid on the horn, flipped on the emergency flashers, and moved into the oncoming traffic lane, which thankfully remained empty.

"Honey," he reminded his wife. "They're criminals with guns. We *don't* want to catch them."

"We have a gun." Lola reached for the shivaree bag which she must have inspected, and spilled the contents across the seat.

"A popgun won't make us any less dead, but if you and your lead foot could get us in front of the kidnappers, I could throw out the smoke bombs in an effort to slow them down."

Herman reached across the console, gathering the smoke bombs, and lighter. He scooted across to the passenger side and rolled down the window to be ready, and then tried to use the lighter with no luck. "Stupid kid-proof lighter."

"Squeeze it on both sides," Lola offered before she goosed the gas pedal, speeding past the van. Squeezing hard, Herman managed a flame on the lighter only to have the wind blow it out. "Good gravy!" He held the lighter below the window and managed to light one smoke bomb, then another off that one. He threw the first one out and continued this process until all six smoke bombs lay fuming on the pavement.

Unfortunately, the process also filled the sedan with acrid smoke, causing both Herman and Lola to cough. The car slowed and moved back into its appropriate lane as the white van swerved around them with a screech of tires. Lola powered down all the windows to rid the vehicle of smoke. Herman rested his hand on his wife's shoulder. "If I want to have a few more years with my beloved, we may have to avoid activities like this."

"Or do more," Lola suggested with a giggle.

Police sirens blared behind them, forcing everyone unceremoniously to the side of the road.

"Looks like the cavalry is on its way." Herman exhaled audibly, feeling the burden of saving Katie slip from his shoulders. After a half-dozen police cars passed, Lola eased back on the road. She went a little farther and turned into a restaurant parking lot and stopped. She asked with a sassy tilt of her head, "How about a cold iced tea to settle your nerves?"

"Sounds good. Maybe a piece of pie to go with it?" Herman

suggested and then eased himself out of the car to open his wife's door.

"Wait." Lola reached for her phone wedged under the passenger seat due to her stunt driving. When she picked up the phone, she noticed it was still on. "Hello?" She listened. "We saw the squad cars go by. We figured it was time to give up the chase. Hubby and I are going to take a snack break. Thank you."

She ended the call and put it in her purse, but the moment she did, it rang. "I wonder who that could be?" Even though she'd just dropped the phone into her bag, despite concentrated rooting, she failed to unearth it and dumped the contents on the seat to find the cell.

"Oh, it's Marcy." She picked up the phone and accepted the call. "Hello?" She held the phone between the two of them so they could both hear.

"Are you two, okay?"

"We're fine," Lola answered, but Herman added, "I may need my car alignment checked, but other than that, we're good. We assume the police nabbed the kidnappers. The center receptionist climbed into the van, too."

"Ah, that's who it was," Marcy exclaimed. "Someone was still at the center, laundering dirty money, but no one could figure out who it was. Once the former director and the accountant bailed, it looked like no one would figure out who was behind it, although there were some suspicions."

"Didn't the accountant die?" Lola inquired.

"That's what he wanted us to think. The former director and accountant were spotted on the airport's close circuit television about a month ago. At the time, they were not wanted for anything and it's not illegal to fly."

"What about faking his own death?" Lola basically growled the words, still whipped up from the car chase.

"Faking your death isn't the problem, but more why you do it. Perhaps a person did it to get out of serving time or paying child support. The pseudo dead guy's wife could collect life insurance, which would be fraud. If he did it to get out of paying taxes, that's all punishable. Let's hope he's in a county that doesn't mind giving them both up."

"Who was investigating? FBI?" Herman asked because as far as he could tell, no one checked out the center or some of its more larcenous employees. No men in suits showed asking pointed questions.

"No, the Treasury Department. Money laundering is their bailiwick. It's not public knowledge, but I think it's okay if you know. It was Ron, which I didn't find out until yesterday evening. He worked on behalf of the Treasury Department, but more in a lone-wolf manner, which probably contributed to the problems. It would have helped a lot if that information had been shared. It explained why they weren't that concerned. The scuttlebutt is Ron chose his own exit—we never expect to see him again. No surprise since he often investigates crime syndicates. Those type carry grudges. It's best for everyone to consider him dead.

Turns out he knows his way around explosives. Not too sure if the garage had been rigged to explode if the culprits got too close, or the explosion could have taken out Ron, too. In the end, a professional made the explosive device since only Ron's rental was damaged and none of the surrounding buildings."

"The fact that Ron knew his explosives will please Gus."

"I'm sure it will."

"One more thing," Herman said. "Ron was Stacey Reuben, but Stacey is listed as dead. What's up with that?"

"Can't say. Don't know. A person who doesn't exist would make a perfect undercover guy, though."

Herman checked his watch. "Well, you'd better go. Have you reached the wedding chapel yet?"

"No. We turned around when we got Lola's misdial. Friends don't let friends chase down kidnappers on their own. Besides, we can get married another day. The important thing for Lance and me is that all my sleuths attend the wedding."

Chapter Thirty

PEOPLE CROWDED INTO the combined lounge as love songs drifted from the nearby stereo. There were a lot of inquiries about the Texas hold 'em tournament that fizzled on its second day, due to three missing finalists. Lola assigned those who didn't move fast enough to a task, from hanging paper wedding bells to setting up chairs. Near the far wall, Gus and Jake worked with a few of the dietary staff members to set up the reception table. Due to the rapidness of the wedding, no wedding cake could be assembled in such a short time. However, the kitchen staff made dozens of chocolate and vanilla iced cupcakes topped with tiny handcuffs. Not the most romantic emblem, but rather appropriate for two cops.

Herman rolled tape to put behind another bell. "Where're Eunice and Hannah? Shouldn't they be helping?"

"They went to get two special guests, Bear and Domino. It's only fitting those two attend. After all, they brought Lance and Marcy together."

Curious about what romantic story his wife had concocted about the cat and tiny dog, he decided to tease her. "Crime brought them together."

"That's how they met," she acknowledged with a nod as she tied a white ribbon around a bouquet of pink rosebuds and baby's breath. "They worked side by side for years, liking and respecting one another, but not making the love connection."

Gus interrupted them to gesture toward the reception table. "Jake wants to put the utensils in the cups working side down. How will people know what they are?"

This must be one of those dilemmas wedding planners faced. Herman laced his fingers together, turned his palms out, and stretched. He winked at Lola to let her know he intended to handle this. "If they were prong up, then everyone would touch them—not sanitary at all."

"Doesn't sound good," Gus admitted and strolled halfway to the table before he shouted back. "We only have forks!"

A resident asked if she could help and soon found herself putting out plastic white swans filled with mints. Another volunteer handled the black swans filled with nuts. Some might think the couple opted for a black and white wedding, but the color scheme resulted from limited supplies in the local discount store. Halloween passed a few weeks ago, which would account for the black items.

Once Lola had assigned the volunteers tasks, she returned to her theory. "Marcy's accident could have shaken something loose in Lance. Perhaps he decided to go for it, but more likely it was his caring for the pets and bringing them to the center for a visit. While we visited with Bear, he caught up with Marcy. Then, when Marcy assumed care of the animals at her house, he visited them because it served as a perfect excuse to show up all the time."

Herman brought his fist up to his chin as he mulled over her reasoning. "At first, I would have thought Bear and Domino had nothing to do with Marcy and Lance getting together, but you've sold me on the four-legged matchmakers."

"Good." She wrapped one arm around her husband for a half-embrace. "Because they're here." Hannah and Eunice entered the room with two animal carriers. A few of the residents, spotting the carriers, ebbed closer, rather like a wave, for a peek at the diminutive pup or the tuxedo cat.

Katie entered the room, escorted by the fresh-faced policeman who'd been so helpful in the aftermath. The single mother still looked fragile but strong enough to show up for the wedding. The residents, unaware of her trauma, greeted her with a smile or commented on her handsome escort, which caused her to blush. Herman wondered how she really was. He whispered into his wife's ear, "What do you think about Katie?"

"It will take time, lots of time, but in the end, she'll be all right." Her shoulders went up in a shrug. "What other choice does she have with a son to look after?"

Sometimes choices were made out of necessity.

BOTH LANCE AND Marcy had arrived at the station the day before to witness the receptionist and Dead Eyes brought into the station. While the man had a long record, the woman didn't, which explained why no one was suspicious of her. Of course, she'd been put in place by the former director, who left her with a stack of deposit slips with instructions to keep putting dirty money into the pet therapy account, where it could be withdrawn at a later date. That explained Dead Eyes and his ilk making appearances at the center.

Once Katie started looking into the pet therapy account, they must have decided she might be an issue, which explained the botched kidnapping attempt. Not yet a hardened criminal, the receptionist conveniently informed on her cohorts.

Part of the fallout from the kidnapping included Lance seeing Marcy in her wedding dress before the ceremony. Hannah came up with some historical facts about the reason the groom wasn't supposed to see the bride before the wedding, because most marriages were arranged using miniatures paintings of the intended which ran to the flattering side. The groom could always back out if the bride's appearance didn't live up to painting, which also explained the modesty veil that covered the bride's face.

By the time Hannah finished her wedding trivia, she stomped out any romance associated with weddings. The happy couple entered the event room with their favorite retired judge in tow.

"Look, they're here!" Lola nudged her husband. "We need to get things done. They've already missed a day on their honeymoon. Good thing they're not flying."

"Where are they going?" Herman asked, realizing he had missed out on much of the wedding plans by concentrating on Ron.

"It's a secret. No one knows." She held up her hand to whisper to her husband. "I think it is because Gus threatened to shivaree them."

"No doubt."

The judge separated from the happy couple and issued directives while the soon-to-be-wed duo stopped in front of Lola and Herman. Marcy nodded at Lola. "I want you to stand up with me. If you want, you can hold Bear as opposed to a bouquet. That way he's a part of the ceremony."

"Thrilled," Lola answered with a wide grin.

Lance addressed Herman with a mischievous twinkle. "I'd like you to stand up with me and you can hold a bouquet if you wish."

"That's all right. Being able to stand with you is an honor. Watching you two youngsters fall in love does my heart good."

Lance bumped his future wife's arm. "Did you hear him call us youngsters?"

"I like it," she smirked. "Well, we need to talk to the rest of the sleuths. When they start playing "Good Luck Charm" by Elvis, that's your cue to assemble by the podium. We'll take all the luck we can get.

A few minutes later, the activity director sat by the stereo, starting and stopping various songs until she found the right one. The Senior Sleuths hurried into place with the men gathered with Lance and the women with Marcy. Eunice draped Marcy's black and white cat over her shoulder, which caused Herman to wince, never being a huge fan of the cat. Wherever Domino appeared, chaos shortly followed.

The judge cleared his throat, a signal he most likely used in the courtroom for attention. "It's my absolute honor and pleasure to join these two fine individuals together. I've known them both for years as they've kept this city safe. They never married or had children—the greatest pleasures known to humankind—since they put their jobs first. I'm thankful they finally woke up and realized you can protect your community *and* have a life, too. No two people deserve each other more." He smiled at both of them and asked, "Do you have vows you'd like to read?"

"We do."

Lance unfolded a piece of paper, cleared his throat, and read. "You are the dream I never dared to believe could exist. You are my sun, my moon, my stars, my reason for living. Marcy, you give my life purpose and structure. I can't imagine living without you in my life."

A few tears were wiped away among the audience. Herman might have grown a little misty-eyed if he hadn't been watching the wiggling cat, knowing in many ways it served as the other boot and would soon drop.

The judge nodded at Marcy, who grinned and said, "Ditto," which caused some laughter. "No, wait! I do have vows." She inhaled deeply. "I promise to take you, Lance, as my husband to honor, love—but not obey. No reason to get crazy here."

They both chuckled, demonstrating they were familiar with each other's vows. Marcy added, "I never expected to fall in love until I met you. Now, I don't know how I existed without you. Stay with me and be my love."

After the tears were wiped away, the judge pronounced them husband and wife, the music swelled, and Domino jumped down and fled the room, just like Herman expected. He might not be Columbo, but he recognized immediately that those two were destined for each other, and that Domino would steal the spotlight—as usual.

The End.

Coming in 2022

The Talking Dog Detective Agency Series

Pawsitively Smokin'
Chapter One

AN URGENT CALL from her investigative partner, Sawyer Donovan, forced an exhausted Nala and Max back into the dusty sedan after a long day of searching for a missing feline. The warmer spring weather and longer days made the open windows Max usually desired not such a hardship. The sight of him with his shaggy dog head out the window and a wide grin as he sniffed the air as they whizzed past various fast-food eateries made Nala chuckle.

"I know. I'm hungry, too. We'll grab some dinner right after we see what Donovan wants." She wiggled her shoulders to loosen them up from their pinched posture created by spending a good part of the day hunched over, peering under bushes for a runaway Persian cat. Fortunately, Max located the wayward cat that had hunkered down under a porch. Not expecting an answer from her canine companion, she continued talking.

"We can hope Donovan rounded something up for us besides background checks on dating hopefuls." Nala sighed heavily, well aware that she'd leaped before she'd looked when deciding to leave the educational world to try her hand at private investigation. She tucked her medium-length, dark hair behind one ear. "You hear me, Max?"

Her rescue shepherd mix pulled his head back into the car, gave an all-over shake, and then replied, "Anything is better than chasing down pampered furballs."

Any other person might have slammed on the brakes or maybe even pinched themselves to assure themselves they weren't dreaming, but not Nala. The former pre-school teacher had adopted Max over a year ago, unaware that the pooch could talk. Her friend Karly, who worked at the shelter, urged her to take him without mentioning his unusual ability. For all the folks who wished their pet could talk, it never turned out as you expected. Max tended to obsess over certain things.

As a pair of familiar arches slipped by them, Max moaned, "Cheeseburger."

"Donovan, first. Cheeseburger, second."

Besides obsessing on cheeseburgers, her pooch, unlike the stoic shepherds who worked as police dogs, swung toward the dramatic side. A woeful howl that started low and increased in volume filled the car. "I'm dying from hunger!"

The screech of sirens forced Nala to check her rearview mirror as she maneuvered her car to the road shoulder to allow the massive fire trucks to hurtle past her. An ambulance could be following.

Max quit complaining and his ears tilted forward in interest. "You know, I could have been a fire dog."

"Uh-huh." Nala double-checked her mirror and slipped back onto the blacktopped road. "They don't use fire dogs anymore."

"What?" Max jerked his head in a classic double take. "Why not?"

Other times, her pet could be like many of her former preschool students—always asking questions. As a former teacher, most people—and one dog—expected her to know the answer to every question. When she didn't, they'd react like she'd disappointed them somehow. However, this subject she knew because preschoolers liked fire dogs, too.

"Fire dogs, or Dalmatians, served as carriage dogs. They ran in front of the carriages, barking to clear the way for the horses. They were early sirens. Once they arrived at the fire, the horses would get skittish around the flames, and the dogs calmed them."

"Cool job." He gave a long howl. "How's that?" he asked with his nose lifted in the air. "Almost siren-like?"

"Certainly loud," Nala acknowledged and rubbed her ear with her free hand. "Remember the car rules. No howling or barking inside the car."

Max dropped his head before pushing out a raspy, "Sorry."

Another turn brought them closer to the aging building where her private investigation office resided. Not the popular part of town, not even the not-so-popular side, but more like the forgotten, tumble-down section, which is why she could handle the rent. Up ahead, the red and white flashing lights of the fire trucks painted the surroundings with a rosy glow.

One firefighter stood in the street, stopping thru traffic. A few vehicles in front of her powered down their windows to debate why they couldn't get through to their destinations. Too far away to hear the outcome, Nala noticed the firefighter gesturing at the sky darkened by gray smoke. With the trucks and the buildings, it made it hard to deduce exactly where the smoke originated. The cars in front of her made a U-turn, with the last one squealing its tires as it sped by her. She might as well park and walk the rest of the way.

"Looks like we're going to have to hoof it."

Max muttered something, but Nala chose not to ask. Knowing him, he probably remarked that walking equaled more food even though the office sat a mere two blocks away. The strident shriek of a police car came from behind. Nala pulled hard to the right, next to the curb. Technically, she'd be parking the wrong way, but she doubted with all the chaos that anyone would be handing out parking fines.

Police usually helped with traffic control, leaving the firefighters to do the important work. The squad car stopped sideways in the intersection to prevent anyone from entering. Nala put up her hand to wave, thinking she might know the cop since so many police passed through their house at one time or another due to her father being a career police member, but she put it down fast. No time to chit-chat or make nice. The officer had a job to do, as did she.

Two sharp barks from Max resulted in the young male officer turning and yelling, "Hey, Max!"

Everyone knew her dog but somehow missed the human at the end of the leash. This must be what it's like to be a chauffeur to celebrities. Her father, Captain Sloane Bonne, thought Max showed an amazing aptitude and could be a police dog, which resulted in his bringing the dog to the academy and running him through police dog exercises. Most were astounded at how quickly he conquered minor challenges, unaware that Nala had prepped him by letting him watch videos of police dogs and coaching him on expected behavior. When your dog could speak and understand English, it made it much easier to get your point across.

Sure, she could have mentioned that Max could speak—she even tried to once, but Max refused to speak, making her look like an idiot. On the whole, it worked better if people didn't know. A con artist could snatch her canine companion in hopes of making the big bucks with the black, shepherd mix. Little would they suspect that, despite his ability to understand commands, he only performed when he wanted to.

The officer strolled over to where Max hung out the window to scratch him behind the ears. He peered at Nala, probably trying to decide if she'd made off with Captain Bonne's dog. Nala opened up the car door slowly and introduced herself. "I'm Nala."

Not a flicker of recognition showed in the officer's eyes, demonstrating how much her father talked about his daughter. Perhaps he hadn't heard her. "Nala? Nala Bonne?"

"Oh…" he stretched out the word. "Are you related to Captain Bonne?"

Was she related? Well, that should definitely confirm how much her father talked about her. Inwardly, she sighed, well aware that her father hoped she'd follow in his footsteps, even to the point of drilling her in observational skills and teaching her how to get out of a chokehold. Still, most parents mentioned their children at some point. After all, he'd had the last thirty years to come up with a sentence or two about her.

"I am." She refused to say any more, embarrassed.

The officer gave her a short nod and then mentioned getting back to work before moving toward his parked vehicle. Nala watched him leave, scooting out of her seat and releasing Max.

When those of the police persuasion discovered a shared bloodline between her and her no-nonsense father, they inevitably mentioned getting back to work, as if she served as some type of performance inspector, ready to radio details back to her father. There was not much she could do about that. The clasp on the leash made a metallic click as she attached it to Max's collar. Once she shouldered her purse, she closed the car door only to realize the passenger window remained open.

Her lips pulled down as she regarded the open window. At the most, they wouldn't be over twenty minutes. Still, the dated sedan had a lot of mileage left on it. For all she knew, it might still be the type of car you could boost by hotwiring it. It would be just her luck—even worse would be calling it in and having her father ask if she'd failed to lock it.

Sighing, she dug the keys out of her purse, leaned inside with her left hand still grasping the lead, turned the engine over, and then powered up the window. "Geesh, look at how much trouble you are."

Any non-talking dog would accept the blame and be on its merry way—or Nala assumed so. "Whatever…" Max managed in a low voice, keeping to his practice of not talking in front of others. The two of them broke into a swift walk to the office. While she wanted to get in and out and finish the day with a hot bath, her pooch focused more on food.

As they turned the corner, their office building stood safe and not on fire, while a derelict warehouse a little farther down fared less well, with flames climbing out of its broken windows. As Nala noted before—not the best part of town. Some of her clients insisted on her visiting them once she gave them her address. More customers equaled more money and a better location.

The emergency personnel ignored them as they scampered up the concrete stairs and pushed the key into the entry door. The doorknob refused to budge. Nala put her weight into the door and jerked the knob upward, which moved the knob a centimeter or so, but not enough to open it. She repeated the process until the door popped open with a groan.

"We seriously need to move," she grumbled as she moved into the dusty hallway. A striking man with lifted eyebrows paused on the steps. *Donovan.* Every time Nala mentioned her partner's name, her best friend, Karly, simpered, which may have been why the man succeeded in areas where Nala could come up with no answer. For Pete's sake! The man could just use his photo on social media and get all the help he wanted, with his thick head of hair and bedroom eyes.

"Oh, it's you guys," Sawyer Donovan remarked as he took the last two stairs. "Thought someone might be trying to break in again."

"It felt like it. I'm surprised no one asked me if I was, with first responders swarming the area."

In the dwindling light, Nala cocked her head, trying to see what about her partner made other women act the fool around him. If they worked with him, they might change their minds about how he'd snag the starring role in a romantic comedy by playing himself. She always knew when her partner came back from his insurance investigation adventures because he exploded into the office. Not a TNT type of explosion, but more papers, clothes, and fast-food containers everywhere, which often contained food to Max's delight.

"I'm glad you're here. I have a case that will light your fire."

Nala closed her eyes. How could a man under forty use such dated expressions? He told dad jokes, too, which probably drew the single mothers like the offer of free babysitting. "Okay, I'll bite. What is it?"

He held a finger to his lips and then motioned for them to retire upstairs to the office. Oh yeah, the man epitomized *secretive*. Sometimes, she wondered if his name even was Sawyer Donovan— even though she'd seen his license. There were plenty of good fake licenses on the open market. She trudged up the stairs as Max raced ahead, well aware that she'd jump at whatever job Donovan planned to throw her way. With any luck, it wouldn't involve peering underneath shrubbery for wayward felines.

Author Notes

This is the place I talk about the inspiration for the story, but this time I'd like to talk about my editor, Larriane Wills, who died from COVID before **Late for the Wedding** reached completion. Here is my tribute to her.

Larriane

Over a decade ago, I became a part of Secret Cravings Publishing. Excitement reigned in our household due to someone believing a story I wrote was good enough to be published. The first step to the publishing route included assigning me an editor, Larriane Wills. And what an editor she was. What initially impressed me about her editing style was her vast storehouse of knowledge. What she didn't know, she could look up either on the Internet or by consulting an expert on the subject. More than a few times her expertise saved me from embarrassing myself in print.

In historical fiction, I wanted my character to use matches, which existed at that time. Larriane pointed out that even though they existed, they weren't in common use in the United States. I wanted my mail-order bride to board a train to meet her soon-to-be husband, but Larriane pointed out that trains didn't go that far at the time. A stagecoach ended up substituting for the train.

Besides her willingness to go the extra mile, I remember Larriane's sweetness and fearlessness—an unusual combination. I considered her fearless because she didn't let things like deafness slow her down. Often, at writing conferences, she used an FM receiver unit to hear the speaker. The speaker might turn away or rattle papers, making it difficult to hear anything, but still, she persevered.

I can't imagine how hard it was for her to travel places—which she did. Travel became more difficult when an oxygen tank became part of her luggage. When security stopped her for not having a doctor's note to travel, she dealt with it, got on the plane, and made it to conference.

Coyotes roamed the edges of her back yard, which forced her to keep a sharp eye on her beloved dogs. When one grabbed her tiny dog, she chased the predator and beat it with her cane until it dropped her pet. Someone needs to make an action hero movie with the lead character named Larriane, and wielding a wicked cane.

Her sweetness showed up in many ways. She loved, loved her family and Christmas because of the joy of the season and family get-togethers. Homemade crafts came from endless hours of stitching. She created crocheted, knitted, or cross-stitched gifts for one and all. Right before she went into the hospital, she either mailed my cross-stitched cup filled with tea or had someone mail it for her.

Despite how diva-like writers could react to her comments, she never reacted in turn. Maybe she understood because she, too, wrote. In my opinion, she must have been an old soul, who held a deeper understanding of the human heart than most. She once told me that her goal was to make the authors better writers. Sure, it would be easy to buzz through a story and make corrections—basically rewriting it—but she didn't do that.

Instead, she wrote on my manuscript about trying a different word, or to elaborate on the scene due to its importance in the timeline. She kept track of time and days in the story and warned me when I made my heroine do more than humanly possible in a day.

Larriane also witnessed the absurdity of life and stored it away to save for another time when she need to smile. She shared tales of her own life in our email exchanges. Life dealt her some severe blows, which never brought her to her knees. The woman I knew could have inspired the warrior princess trope. Deafness, age, coyotes, and diva writers couldn't take the wind out of her sails.

Besides being my editor, I thought of Larriane as my friend, and encourager. She used her social media presence to promote other writers all the time. In a way, I never wanted to think of being without Larriane—so I didn't. Unfortunately, COVID had other plans, and her indomitable will finally folded. This isn't goodbye because she lives on in her books with the pen names Larriane Wills and Larion Wills. She endures in all the authors she guided. There is, in the end, her family, her dearest treasure.

www.ingramcontent.com/pod-product-compliance
Lightning Source LLC
Chambersburg PA
CBHW051954220626
47052CB00004B/938